12/17

My
Brigadista
Year

My Brigadista Year

KATHERINE PATERSON

CANDLEWICK PRESS

This story is for my dear friends
Emilia Gallego,
who was a true Conrado Benítez Brigadista,
and her friend and mine,
Isabel Serrano.

Copyright © 2017 by Minna Murra, Inc.
Map on pages viii–ix copyright © 2017 by Mike Reagan

First edition 2017

Library of Congress Catalog Card Number pending
ISBN 978-0-7636-9508-8

17 18 19 20 21 22 BVG 10 9 8 7 6 5 4 3 2 1

Printed in Berryville, VA, U.S.A.

This book was typeset in ITC Mendoza Roman.

Candlewick Press
99 Dover Street
Somerville, Massachusetts 02144

visit us at www.candlewick.com

It is the duty of man to raise up man.

— José Martí

Contents

GULF OF MEXICO

FLORIDA

MIAM

KEY WEST

VARADERO BEACH

HAVANA

CIENFUEGOS

BAY OF PIGS

CARIBBEAN SEA

HAVANA

LORA'S APARTMENT

LORA'S SCHOOL

SIMÓN BOLÍVAR AVENUE

ESCAMBRAY MOUNTAINS

MANUEL ASCUNCE
MURDERED HERE ⊗

PALMARITO COFFEE FARM

ACOSTAS' FARM

← ROAD TO
CIENFUEGOS

MILITIA CAMP

THE PIG ROAST

SANTANAS' FARM

⊗ CONRADO BENÍTEZ
MURDERED HERE

MEETING CAMP

LORA ENTERS THE FOREST

MILES

0   5   10   15

ATLANTIC OCEAN

ESCAMBRAY
MOUNTAINS

CUBA

LORA'S CUBA

N

MILES

0   50   100

CHAPTER ONE

The Campaign

HAVANA, MARCH 1961

"Ai—ee!" In all my thirteen years, I hadn't heard a screech like that since the time I accidentally stepped on the cat's tail. But now it was my own mama's voice, shrieking to high heaven.

My father, usually so quiet, wasn't much better. He was shaking his head and pacing like a caged lion. "No! No! No! Lora! Lora! Lora! This is unheard of. *What* were you *thinking?*"

At that moment, I was thinking that he was about to tear my permission sheet to shreds. Instead he crumpled it in his hand and threw it into the waste can. "Now. No more of this nonsense." He gave me a pat on the top of my head and nodded at my mother, who hushed her cries. "Your grandmother is resting."

But it was too late. Abuela was standing at the door, her hair still disheveled from her nap, her face crumpling into a thousand new wrinkles.

"What is it, Paulo?" she asked. "What is unheard of?"

"This, this . . ." my father began.

"My baby. . ." my mother injected, her tears threatening to start all over again.

"This granddaughter of yours," my father said to Abuela, with a stern look to the side at my mother, *"this granddaughter of yours* thinks we will let her throw away her life."

"That's hard to believe, Lora," Abuela said to me. She began to wrap her kerchief about her head. Her gray hair was thin, and she liked to cover the balding. She looked so tiny, so fragile. I didn't want to distress her.

"I don't want to throw away my life, Abuela, truly I don't. I want to—"

"You have no idea—" my father began, but Abuela put up her small hand.

"Why don't we all sit down—you, too, Paulo—and then Lora can explain to me quietly and calmly just what's going on. I don't like my siesta disrupted, much less the peace of my family."

The three of us waited until Abuela had finished tucking under the tail end of her kerchief and seated herself comfortably in her rocker. My parents plunked down on the sofa, and I took the low stool near Abuela's chair.

"Now," she said, looking straight at me, "suppose you explain how you're planning to throw away your life."

"She thinks—" my father started.

"Hush. I'm asking Lora."

"Abuela, you remember how last fall our leader told the United Nations that Cuba would become a literate nation in one year?" I asked.

She nodded. "Yes, he said that."

"We're really going to do it, Abuela. We really are! And—and I want to be a part of it."

Papi leaned forward, about to interrupt, but once again Abuela raised her hand. "How do you want to help, Lora?"

"Well, today there was a poster at school. The government is calling on all of us who can read and write to teach the citizens who don't know how. The poster said—"

"That doesn't mean," Papi said, "that the government expects thirteen-year-old girls, who have never left their homes, whose parents care for and protect them—"

"If the government is not seeking young girls, why is there a poster in a girls' secondary school?" Abuela asked.

"It doesn't make sense," he muttered.

"What did the poster say, Lora?"

"It called for young men and women to join an army of young literacy teachers. It said: 'The home of a family of campesinos who cannot read or write is waiting for you now. Don't let them down!'"

"And what made you think the call was for you, Lora?"

"I can read and write — really I'm quite a good student. Shouldn't I share what I have with someone who needs it? Isn't that what you've always said, Papi? That we children should share what we have with those less fortunate?"

"I didn't mean —"

"Your parents have taught you well, Lora. We *are* called on to share what we have with those less fortunate."

"But the child has no idea how primitive conditions are in the country. There's no electricity. There is no running water —" my father began, only to be interrupted by Mama.

"I've heard that those campesinos don't even have proper *toilets.*" It was hard to ignore the anguish in my mother's voice.

"You've hardly ever been out of Havana . . ." Papi added.

"You've never spent a night away from home, not even at my mother's house," Mama wailed.

Abuela heard out their complaints before she turned to me. "It will be a hard life," she said. "Your father is right. You can't imagine how hard."

"I know," I said, but of course, I knew nothing except that I wanted to be a part of the campaign. The girl in the poster was wearing a uniform. I looked at her smiling face and for the first time in my life imagined what it might feel like to be truly free. No one telling me not to play in the sun or mess up my nice dress. I didn't want to spend the next few years of my life just sitting still so that someday I would be able to make a proper marriage. I wanted to do something, be someone.

My father stood up. "Do you want to throw away your life?"

"No. I want to live it."

"And break your mother's heart?"

"No, no, Papi. I want to make you both proud of me."

"They killed that boy." He muttered the words as he sat down heavily, his head in his hands. My heart gave a jerk. We all knew the story of the young literacy worker who was killed by the bandidos in January.

For a long time, or what seemed a long time to me, no one said anything. Finally Abuela leaned forward and put her small hand on my shoulder, but she was looking at Papi. "Remember, Paulo, how we have longed and prayed for a new day in our country?" she said. "Well, that new day, the one we prayed for, the one your brother died for, is here." I was looking at my grandmother, not at Papi, but the sigh he gave was deeper than a sob.

Abuela was quiet for a minute and then went on: "With a new day, my son, must come new people. We who are old must learn from the young how to change." She stroked my shoulder. "I know it will be hard, Lora, harder than you can ever imagine. So. Will you promise to come home if it is too hard?"

I nodded.

She studied my face as though she were reading my heart. Finally she spoke. "Is there something that needs to be signed?"

"Papi refuses."

She sighed. "Then I suppose *I* must. Get it for me."

I didn't dare look at my parents. I fetched the wadded-up slip out of the trash and smoothed it out on a book. Then I got a pen and handed the paper and pen to my grandmother, but at that point Papi stood up. "Lora, do you truly promise me to come home if it proves too hard?"

"I promise."

He held out his big hand. "Then give the paper to me. It's better if I sign. I am your father."

I could hear my mother gasp, but I kept my eyes on my grandmother's smile.

Chapter Two

Back to the Beginning

HAVANA, 1947–1958

Even though, with Abuela's help, I won the fight to join the campaign, I was shaken. I never liked to oppose my father, and I always felt bad when I did. My mother was another matter. She had such ideas of what a girl should be. My little brothers, Silvio and Roberto, could fight like alley cats and my mother would only smile. But should I get involved in a fight with them? *Watch out!* I was not being ladylike. They could play out all day in the summer sun, but I must come in after a few minutes for fear of ruining my beautiful complexion.

My first three years were blissful. I was an adored only child — and the only grandchild on either side of the family. Then *boom!* Everything changed overnight when my brother Silvio was born. For one thing, my mother's mother was so thrilled, you would have thought heaven had come down to earth. Her own son, Pedro, was too much of a playboy to think about marriage, and my mother had so far only given her a granddaughter. After Silvio was born, Grandmother began to insist that we come across the city to visit her every Sunday. I hated those visits. I could never understand why my mother would make me go as well. *That* grandmother paid no attention to me at all with her darling Silvio to cradle in her arms and coo at.

By the time Silvio was walking around and talking, I began to tell him what he should do, as I firmly believed was my right, but if my mother heard me ordering Silvio to give me his cookie, she would scold me. My pride was injured. I was the eldest, and he was only a baby. Of course he ought to obey me. I wasn't bossy; I *was* the boss. I almost had him convinced of this fact, when *whammo!* Roberto was born. Silvio quickly decided that now *he* was the boss. And my mother encouraged him. "You are now the big brother," she would tell him. One day I reminded him that he was not as big as I, and he put his hands on his hips, threw back his head, and declared, "But you are only a *girl!*" So of course I hit him. He cried. And my mother gave me a smack. I took the cat to my bed and cried.

The year I was born, Papi's father had died and my parents and I had moved in with Abuela. Since before I could remember anything, I had slept in the same room with her, and we were very close. But when I complained to her that time about how unfair my mother had been, even Abuela scolded me for hitting my brother.

I have always known that Abuela loves me, but she always has had a special place in her heart for Roberto. This is because her son Roberto, my father's younger brother, was one of the young men killed in what is known as the 26th of July uprising against General Batista. My brother was born the following month, and so was named after the uncle he would never meet.

I was, of course, as jealous of a baby as a five-year-old could possibly be. But even I could sense that Abuela needed that baby in her time of grieving, so I kept my thoughts to myself, unless you count my whispers to the cat while squeezing him until he yowled and wriggled out of my arms.

I might have been jealous, but I didn't hate my brothers. When there were no grown-ups to interfere, we often played happily together. Also, I had one magic spell with which to charm the little imps: I could read fluently. When I read them a story, they would sit almost still and listen. "Read it again," they would beg. And I would.

We were not a wealthy family. Our apartment was small. In Abuela's bedroom, I slept on a cot, and my parents had the other bedroom. My brothers shared a small cot in the corner of the living room.

You would think that wouldn't work, but those boys could sleep through a revolution — and they did.

Before the revolution, my mother worked as a maid in one of the big hotels run by the criminals that people in the United States call the Mafia. Our dictator, Batista, was not only a great friend to those American crooks, he also raked huge profits for himself from their hotel and casino operations in our country. Mama hated the hotel work because the rich tourists who came there to drink and gamble were so nasty to the help. They seldom left a tip for the maid, and the wages were hardly worth the bus ride, but it was a job, and in those days, jobs were hard to come by. My father worked as a tailor in a shop more than two miles from our apartment. He always walked to work to save the bus fare.

So when I said that I wanted to go to one of the best and therefore one of the most expensive girls' secondary schools in Havana, my mother looked at me as though I'd lost my mind. My father shook his head sadly. He wanted me to have more education than he did, but why one of the most expensive schools in the city? He couldn't possibly . . .

My mother burst in. "What are you thinking, Lora? That your poor parents should beggar themselves only to let you become one of those clever people who will look down their long noses on those who love you?" She began to cry.

It was then that Abuela stepped in, not for the first time. The evening after that particularly bitter exchange with my parents, she took me into our shared bedroom, where she opened a dresser drawer and brought out a small leather case.

"I was saving these to give you on your fifteenth birthday," she said, opening the case to reveal a pair of intricately filigreed gold earrings nestled in the dark-blue velvet lining. The gold gleamed under the ceiling light.

Abuela could see my look of wonder. There was no way I could hide it. "Yes," she said. "They are very precious. They were my quinceañera gift from my own abuela. I didn't have a daughter of my own, so I have saved them for you."

"For me?" I could hardly breathe.

"That was my intent," she said. "But the choice is yours."

What could she mean, the choice was mine?

She went on to explain. "The North American tourists love this old gold jewelry. If I sell these, you can go to any secondary school you wish, but you will not have a special gift from me on your quinceañera."

It was impossible to make such a choice. I was only ten years old. I had never seen anything so beautiful before in my young life, and those earrings were meant for me. I knew my parents would never be able to give me anything approaching such a gift when I turned fifteen. And they had come down from my abuela's abuela. How could I give them up to some arrogant, rich North American tourist? But . . . if I chose the school, I would be prepared for university. With a university education, I would not spend the rest of my life cleaning hotel rooms in a casino. So, in the end, I chose the school.

CHAPTER THREE

My Secondary School

HAVANA, 1958–1959

For the first few weeks, I wondered if I had made the right choice. The teachers seemed contemptuous of my primary-school education. I was sure they sensed that neither of my parents had ever gone past primary school. My new school started with kindergarten, and most of the students there had begun attending it when they were five. I struggled to catch up, especially in math and English.

Many of the nuns who taught us had degrees from England and Europe. Our French maestra had a degree from the Sorbonne University, in Paris, and the Sister who taught English had graduated from Oxford University, in England. They were scholars, and, if I may say so, not as humble as you might imagine a nun should be. Even though I was afraid of them, I was thrilled to hear them speak. But I never raised my hand and hardly raised my voice — the few times a teacher ever noticed me or asked me a question.

Then one day, Sister Evangelina, who taught our national Cuban history and literature, began talking about José Martí.

"I'm sure every one of you girls knows that José Martí is Cuba's greatest revolutionary hero, but how many of you know his literary work?"

Every hand shot up. Even mine.

"Good. Now who will volunteer to recite a favorite poem?"

She waited. No hands went up. "No one?" She sniffed. "You claim to know his work, but none of you has taken the trouble to learn any of it by heart?" She glared around the room. "You disappoint me. I would have expected more from persons with your privileged backgrounds." The only sound breaking the silence was Sister's foot tapping under her habit as she waited. "None of you?"

Slowly and hesitantly, I did something I'd never done before in any of my classes: I raised my hand to volunteer an answer. Sister's bushy eyebrows shot up to the rim of her headdress, but, surprised or not, she called my name.

"'I Grow a White Rose,'" I said in a shaky voice.

"Indeed?"

I don't know where I got the courage, but I stood up and recited the poem. When I sat down, a girl named Norma began to clap. A couple of girls joined in. Then it seemed that the whole class had broken into applause. Eventually, so did Sister Evangelina. I know my face was scarlet, but I could feel a smile stretching across it.

I'd noticed Norma before, but we'd never spoken. The expression on her dark face was always guarded, her almost-black eyes unreadable, but at lunchtime she sidled up to the table where I, as usual, was eating alone. Her face was alive, her eyes sparkling. "'The White Rose' is my favorite, too," she said. "I could have recited it. But I'm not brave like you."

"Would — would you like to sit down?" I was stammering. I wanted a friend so badly.

She smiled and nodded. She sat down across from me and unwrapped an empanada stuffed with meat. I was glad that my thin sandwich with its paper-thin slice of ham was nearly gone.

She took a large bite and began talking, her mouth so full that little bits of meat and bread escaped to the table between us. "I love 'The White Rose.' But this is the first time I've ever told anyone. I can't even talk about José Martí at home. My father doesn't like him. And he especially hates 'The White Rose.' Papá thinks caring about your enemy is weakness. Especially in a man."

Mama, I knew, would have suggested a different friend. Norma's complexion made me sure she was of mixed African blood. And if even my good mama was so biased, Norma surely felt the prejudice of all our fair-skinned classmates. She wiped her mouth with the side of her hand. "I'm so glad there's some-one I can talk about Martí's writing with." *Or any-thing else,* I thought. She took another large bite. "He is a great poet. We should all memorize his poetry, don't you think?"

I quickly forgave Norma's table manners. Here was the friend I'd longed for. We ate together every noon. I soon learned that she, too, had younger brothers whom she both loved and resented. It made me feel that it might be natural for sisters to have such mixed feelings. I told her my mother wanted a daughter who was much more concerned about her looks, and she told me her mother bewailed the fact that Norma's skin was much more like that of her father's family than her own proud family's. When we had known each other for several weeks, she whispered across the lunch table that her father was part of General Batista's bodyguards. But I never told her that my uncle was killed in the 26th of July raid on the Moncada Barracks. That was a family secret I could not share even with my best friend. We swapped poems and gossip, but there was no trading of political views. Just as I couldn't speak of my family's past, she seemed equally hesitant to speak of her family's present.

On New Year's Day 1959, our family, including my other grandmother, was sitting around the holiday meal when the telephone rang. We looked at one another. Who could be calling? But my other grandmother cried, "Answer it, Paulo! It's Pedro calling to wish me a good new year!" She jumped to her feet. She was always sure her son would remember her sometime other than when he needed to pay off his gambling debts.

Papi got up and went to the phone. "Yes . . . No! . . . What? . . . Are you sure? How can you be sure? . . . No! . . . You never . . ." It went on like that until, at last, the one-sided conversation seemed to be over, but Papi just stood there as though stunned, shaking his head in disbelief.

"Is it Pedro? Is he all right?" His alarmed mother cried.

"No." Papi turned toward our anxious faces.

"No, it's not Pedro." The dead phone was still hanging in his hand. "It's . . . it's the General."

"What's that scoundrel done now?" Abuela asked.

"Shhh." My other grandmother always wanted us to be careful. She was sure there was a policeman listening behind every door.

My father continued standing there, the phone in his hand. "Nothing. . . . That is, maybe . . . everything."

He looked at our puzzled faces. "That was Ramón." Papi's best friend. "The General resigned last night. He's — he's fled the country. The 26th of July rebels have taken Santa Clara, and they are on the way here to take charge of the government."

"What? Here? To Havana?" Mama was as puzzled as we all were.

"Fidel is leading them."

"But he's dead," I said. That's what all the newspapers had been saying for years.

"Apparently not," Papi said. He looked at the phone in his hand, as if suddenly seeing it. He turned and hung the phone back on the wall. "Ramón knows these things. He's one of them. That's why he's been disappearing in that car of his. He's been smuggling arms into the Sierra Maestra." He shook his head. "My best friend since elementary school, and he couldn't trust me enough to tell me."

"He didn't want you to know," Abuela said gently. "He was trying to keep you safe, Paulo. He knows the police watch our family."

Papi looked at Abuela, and she looked at him. There was a silence between them that somehow held in it the story of my uncle Roberto's life and sacrifice.

In that quiet moment, we could hear the cheering from the street outside. The news had spread. The boys and I jumped up from the table. "You haven't finished your dinner!" Mama yelled after us, but who cared about food on a day like this? It was more than we could take in. The dictator was gone! The July 26th movement had *not* been destroyed, as all the news reports had claimed. Somehow a tiny band of fighters in the Sierra Maestra had conquered

Batista's army. Fidel Castro was alive and, at that very moment, riding triumphantly toward our city!

As we rushed out the door, I heard Abuela say, right out loud, "Gracias a Dios." Thank God.

The boys wanted to race down the front steps to join the crowds that were flowing like a river in flood toward the main plaza, but I grabbed them by the backs of their shirts. They were likely to be trampled in the excitement. "Wait!" I ordered. "We can't leave here without Papi!"

Soon Papi came out and insisted we come inside. "Your mama has made a beautiful dinner. Come in and finish eating."

"We want to see, Papi," Silvio whined.

"Please, Papi. Can't we go see?"

"There's nothing to see now, boys. Not until they actually get here."

Shouldn't we celebrate our victory for one more day, at least? Although the three of us protested, Mama insisted that we go to school on Monday. It seemed strange that our daily lives should go on as usual—just as if the whole world had not been turned upside down.

And it had been turned upside down. My quiet school was like a swarm of bees whose hive has been disturbed. Even the stoical Sisters seemed agitated.

In every class there were empty seats. *Their parents let them stay home to celebrate!* I thought jealously, until I realized when I went into Sister Evangelina's classroom for Cuban History and Literature that one of the empty seats was Norma's. Her family would not be celebrating. Norma's father was one of the General's bodyguards. Where was she? It was several days before I learned that victory, too, demands a price. I had to accept the fact that Norma and her family had fled north with the General. The revolution had cost me my best friend.

There was no school on January 8. Or if there was, we didn't know about it, because Papi, the boys, and I were among the thousands on Simón Bolívar Avenue, waving our little flags and screaming with joy. We couldn't see over the heads of the crowds. The boys fought for turns on Papi's shoulders and each got a glimpse of the parade of jeeps and trucks left behind by Batista's fleeing army, now carrying our triumphant heroes into the capital.

CHAPTER FOUR

Preparing to Leave

HAVANA, MARCH 1961

Within a week after I submitted my permission and application, I was notified of my acceptance. My mother started weeping all over again, but she knew she was defeated, so she began to plan my wardrobe. "We can't afford any new clothes," she mourned. She always wanted her children to look properly cared for.

"I won't need new clothes, Mama. We'll be wearing uniforms."

That turned on the tear spigot again. The idea of her only daughter in men's clothes was almost too much for her. I put my arm around her shoulder. "It's okay, Mama. I'll still be your daughter."

She looked at me through her tears. "I knew we should never have let you go to that fancy school. You got all sorts of crazy, modern ideas there."

"Oh, Mama, those nuns were dressed head to toe in medieval habits. They didn't give me any crazy, modern ideas." Except, I knew, they had taught me to think for myself. To Mama, that was a crazy, modern idea. Other schools for girls in Havana were often intent only on turning their students into good housewives and mothers.

"Just get me an extra toothbrush and more toothpaste, please. My old comb and brush will do, and I won't be wearing any makeup, you'll be glad to know." Mama thought no girl should wear makeup *or* think about boys before her fifteenth birthday. I didn't dare ask her how old she was before she began thinking about boys. When she seemed so sad that the only new thing in my suitcase was a toothbrush,

I relented and let her make me a new nightgown — cut down from one of her own nice ones.

Papi gave me a camera and three rolls of film. "It's a simple one," he said, "but it takes good pictures. Take care of it, Lora. It belonged to your uncle Roberto." I was touched that he would give me this treasure — one of the few mementos of his lost brother.

I tried to comfort my parents with the fact that after I returned, they would never have to pay another school fee for me. Really. The government had promised that every young volunteer who finished the year of service would be guaranteed free secondary school and university education. Although they never admitted as much, I could tell both of my parents were relieved to hear that bit of news.

Of course, everyone at school knew who had enlisted in the campaign. For the first time I became a center of attention — not all of it positive. "Don't your parents even care about your safety?" one of the senior girls asked me. "What good do you think you can really do? Those campesinos all have IQs below normal. They won't be able to learn. My uncle knows. He was an overseer on a sugar plantation before the revolution."

But at least some of the girls were openly envious and told me so. "I wanted to join, but my papi wouldn't agree. How did you get your parents to sign?" they would ask. When I said that my abuela convinced them, their eyes would go wide with surprise. *Their* grandmothers would never have done such a thing, and I was aware that my abuela was a rare human being — an old woman with young ideas. It made me very proud.

My teachers reacted in different ways. Sister Evangelina urged me to take poems and essays by José Martí to share with every campesino I worked with, so that they would be inspired by our true revolutionary hero. My English maestra demanded to know what I was going to do to keep from going backward in my progress in the language. "There won't be anyone there with whom you can speak English," she said, indicating that by leaving her tutelage, I was leaving civilization and in danger of becoming a barbarian. And the Sister who instructed us in belief and practice took me aside and gave me a little sermon. Teaching literacy was not a bad thing—far from it—but she understood that the young literacy teachers also would be charged with spreading the message of socialism. I was to beware of helping spread secular propaganda—not that socialism was necessarily bad, but when it veered toward the Russian variety, it made an idol of socialist belief and forgot God. "Do not forget God, Lora," she said.

"I won't, Sister," I said, wondering why she thought I might.

"And don't forget the moral teachings of the church."

"Of course not, Sister."

"You will be a young woman alone, unprotected by your father and far from our Mother Church, out there in the countryside. I cannot understand why your parents . . ." She stopped midsentence and sighed before she continued her homily. "Be on your guard against men with sweet words and evil intent.

God will be watching." Even though her voice was stern, if not frightening, I could see her concern for me in her dark eyes.

"I will be very careful, Sister."

"I will pray for you, my child."

"Thank you, Sister," I said, and I meant it. Perhaps I should have said that I would pray for her, because, as it turned out, in just a few months' time, an act was passed to nationalize all the schools, and the teaching of religion there was prohibited.

I found it touching that my brothers were concerned as well.

"But who will read to us after you're gone?"

I put my arm around little Roberto. "You can read by yourself now," I said. "You don't need me anymore."

"Yes, I do," he said through his tears. "I just stumble through the hard words. None of the words are hard for you." He snuffled. "You read better than a teacher. When you read, I see all the pictures in my head and hear the voices."

I stroked his hair and sighed. I would miss him.

Silvio sat up straighter on his chair. "I will read while Lora is gone."

"See?" I said. "Silvio will read in my place."

"He's not as good as you," Roberto protested. "He can't make the voices right."

"I can, too! I just haven't had enough practice." Silvio looked to me for confirmation.

"That's right," I said. "Silvio will get better every day, and by the time I get back, he will read better than me." I said these words as bravely as I could, but there was a hollow echo in my heart. What if they *did* get along just fine without me? What if I was gone so long that they forgot to miss me and filled in the spot where I should have been with other things? They were just little boys, after all, and half the time they were so busy with their own games and spats that they hardly noticed me even when I was standing five feet from them.

Roberto seemed to sense my anxiety. "Silvio will never be as good a reader as you, Lora," he said, and snuggled closer to me on the couch.

For once, Silvio didn't argue, but his stricken face made me forget my fears. "Silvio will read in his own way. And his way will be a very good one," I said.

Silvio nodded his thanks. "Keep going," he said. "We need to finish this book before you leave."

Abuela was especially gentle with me those two weeks before my departure. One night we were both lying on our beds in our dark room, not quite ready for sleep, and she began for the first time to talk to me about her son Roberto, who had given his life for the revolution.

"My son died with a gun in his hand," she said, her voice as soft as the spring night. "As much as I wanted a new day for our country, it has always saddened me that it had to come with brothers killing brothers. I am so glad that instead you will be bringing in the new day with books and pencils and the gift of words.

"I remember," she went on, "the day you discovered you could read. You were only a tiny little thing. We were at the market shopping, and suddenly you let go of my hand. I looked down, startled, but you were turned away, staring at a sign at the fruit seller's. 'Mango!' you said. I thought you were pointing at the fruit, but you grabbed my hand and pointed it at the sign above the fruit. 'It says *mango*, like in my book!' From then on, there was no stopping you. I was very proud."

"I don't remember," I said. "I can't remember when I couldn't read."

"No," she said. "I suppose not. You were very young."

When the time came for me to leave, she didn't go to the station with me. She kissed me on both cheeks and told me to be strong and kind. I promised that I would try. "And I will always wear the rosary you gave me," I said. "That will help me to remember when I forget."

"Good," she said, and kissed me on my forehead. "I will pray for you every night."

CHAPTER FIVE

Varadero Training Camp

APRIL 1961

Those of us who had volunteered from my school had been allowed to take our exams a week early so that we could be at the Varadero training camp when it opened in April. A great herd of buses left the station that morning, so I soon lost sight of my family in the mob of relatives and friends waving farewell to the departing volunteers.

I was not the youngest person on our bus to Varadero Beach. There were at least two boys whom

I guessed were no more than ten or eleven, or about the age of my brother Silvio, though with boys it is hard to guess. When I boarded, I had recognized two other girls from my school and waved shyly. They beckoned me to join them and slid over so we could share one seat. The girls were a class ahead of me, but that day it didn't matter. Old cliques and snobberies were forgotten. Our new selves were one united whole, ready to fight for literacy among the illiterate peasantry.

For most of the one-hour bus ride east along the northern coast, my schoolmates and I covered our nervousness by arguing as to whose family had cried the loudest when the bus left the Havana station. Eventually I was declared winner of the contest because both of my little brothers were wailing and my father was wiping his eyes as well. The girls and I couldn't be too frightened when we were laughing so hard.

From the windows of the bus, I got my first glimpse of Varadero Beach. It was a warm April morning, and at the skyline, where the sea met the bright blue of the spring sky, the water was a dark, almost purplish blue. As it neared the beach, it turned to aquamarine, but then, where the white waves licked the gleaming sand, the water was the color of turquoise. No wonder that before the revolution, rich people from all over had gathered here to play in these beautiful waters and bask in our warm Cuban sun.

It was hard for me to believe that this place that had once been a playground for the wealthy was now the place where we ordinary youngsters would be trained to be brigadistas. We were called brigadistas because we young literacy workers, those of us under eighteen, would be part of the new Conrado Benítez Brigade. It was to be like an army of young people — not an army carrying weapons of war, but, as Abuela had said, one carrying pencils and books.

Conrado Benítez was a young black man who had gone to work as a literacy teacher in the Escambray Mountains. Even though the revolution had triumphed more than a year before, it was still a dangerous place. Some of the defeated army had fled to those mountains with their weapons, determined to defeat the proposed literacy campaign. Just three weeks before Conrado's eighteenth birthday, the insurgents captured him. They tortured him, and then this year, on the fifth of January, to be exact, they killed him. Papi had, of course, thought of his death when I said I wanted to volunteer. Whenever the thought had come into my mind, I'd tried to bury it in my excitement for the adventure ahead.

But I could not, should not, forget Conrado's sacrifice. He was our hero and our example, though secretly I hoped I would never have to follow that example. For all my fierceness in front of my family, I wasn't born to be a hero.

At last our bus pulled off the seaside highway into the parking area behind a hotel that looked to be the size of several soccer fields. When we climbed off the bus, a young man with a clipboard looked up my name and directed me to my lodgings at the resort.

I stood uncertainly in the doorway of a room that I was sure had been once part of a luxurious suite, but which was now filled with cots like a dormitory. One of my roommates saw me before I saw her. "Welcome," she said, taking my small bag from my hand. "Let's find you an empty bed so you can get settled."

What a beautiful girl! That was my first thought. She could have been a poster girl for the campaign, with very light tan skin — reminding me of the milky coffee Abuela made for me on the nights before exams. The green beret on her head made her hazel eyes look almost green, her hair was a lustrous dark brown, and her figure, even in boots and uniform, was a match for any Hollywood star.

While she helped me spread my cot with the simple bedding we had been provided, we exchanged names and told each other where we were from. Marissa was from Santiago de Cuba, but she went to the university in Havana, so we knew some of the same places in the city. *She had left university to join the campaign!* She didn't even need her looks to make me admire her. I so longed to go to university, and here was someone willing to leave that cherished opportunity behind to be part of the Conrado Benítez Brigade with kids like me.

"Have you been here at Varadero long?" I asked, as she seemed to know so much.

She laughed. "Only two days, but they keep us so busy we think we have been here for weeks. They only excused us from class minutes ago so we could help the newcomers piling off the buses. How many of you were there? It looked like thousands of you."

"I don't know how many," I said. "But at the station I'd never seen so many people getting on buses in my life, and all of the buses seemed to be headed for Varadero."

"That's great!" She flashed a beautiful smile. "The campaign needs hundreds of thousands of teachers if we're to get this job done."

"But—" I hesitated.

"You're worried?"

"I can read well and write reasonably well, but I have no idea how to teach anyone else. I'm afraid . . ."

"No, no, you don't have to be afraid, Lorita.

That's why we're all here. We can read and write, but we don't know how to teach someone else how to do what seems so natural to us."

"That's exactly why I'm afraid," I said, not minding at all that she had used the diminutive of my name. She already felt like my older sister.

"Believe me, Lorita, the master teachers won't let you go out into the countryside until they've crammed the how-tos of teaching literacy into that beautiful little head of yours."

Marissa was so wise and kind in a way that none of the real teachers were, but she had told me to pay close attention, and so I did. After all, my life as a brigadista depended on it.

The master teacher of our group had to cram a lot in my "little head." On that first day he gave each of us two books. One was a teachers' manual called *Alfabeticemos,* or *Let's Be Literate.* In this book were passages we brigadistas would read aloud to encourage our students. The second was the book for the students called *Venceremos,* or *We Shall Prevail.* The students' primer had been carefully researched, he told us, so that the first words the student would learn to read would be words that mattered to him or her and to the building of our new nation.

There was a picture before each lesson. One was of three farmers taking a break to chat about their work. Another showed young people planting trees in a deforested area. Then there was one of a fisherman showing off his day's catch. We were told to begin each lesson by using the pictures to encourage a discussion among the students. And we were *never* to act like arrogant authorities, no matter how our own teachers at home had behaved. The textbook was called *We Shall Prevail* for a reason, he said. We, as teachers, would be working together in a common cause with those who were our students. "You will be learning, too," the master teacher said. "Never forget that. You must be courteous, and, above all, respectful and open to all the things your students will teach you."

"Suppose someone doesn't want to learn to read?" a young man asked.

"Then you must not be impatient. You must slowly win him over."

A girl near me asked, "What if a man doesn't want a young girl for a teacher?" That was my question, too, but I felt then as I did during those first months of secondary school: too shy to ask any questions for fear I'd betray my ignorance.

"That may be a real problem for some of you," he said, looking around at the large room full of young people, more than half of us girls. "You girls will have to win them over as friends first. As you work beside them in the fields and in their homes, learning what they can teach you, I believe they will come to realize that you have something valuable to teach them as well. You have been taught in your own homes to respect the authority of your fathers. Respect these men as though they are your fathers; never use a voice of authority with them. Work hard, be cheerful. Teach their children, their wives, whoever in the household is willing to learn. I think the fathers will come to see that they do not want to be left behind."

I felt a pang, remembering once more how I had

flaunted my papi's authority—how reluctantly he had signed his name to the permission sheet.

The master teacher explained every page of the students' manual to us so that we could explain it clearly to our students. Other authorities gave lectures on agriculture—most of us had never seen sugar cane growing in a field or oxen pulling a plow. Now we were to be working beside the farmers who cultivated the land and provided the food that we had always taken for granted when it appeared each day on our dining-room tables. At our home in Havana, as poor as we felt we were, my mother paid an even poorer neighbor to wash our clothes. In the country, *we* would be the washerwomen and, to my horror, the doctors, too! A nurse taught us basic first aid, because the nearest real doctor might be many hours away.

"I hope I'm never called to administer first aid," I said to Marissa. "I've never even put a plaster on one of my little brothers when he skinned his knees. Suppose something dreadful happens."

"There you go, Lorita, imagining all sorts of

catastrophes. Something may indeed happen, but I'm wagering that if or when it does, you'll be up to the challenge."

She saw the doubt in my eyes and laughed her wonderful laugh. "First of all, you must take that look of gloom off your face. Stand up straight and confront head-on whatever it is. Just standing taller will make you feel more confident."

"Really?"

"Try it!"

I straightened up. I did feel more confident.

"And that smile of yours is the greatest asset you have. Don't forget to include that."

I had been in Varadero less than a week when the disastrous news came like the roaring of a hurricane wind on a cloudless day. Three of our airfields had been attacked by planes with insignia painted on them to make it seem they were part of our own air force.

As soon as I had a free moment, I raced to find Marissa.

"What's going on?" I asked her. I needed someone to make sense of the bombing. Bombs belonged in huge world wars in Europe and Asia, not on our island.

"I'm not sure," she said. "But Batista no longer has an air force. Those must have been planes from the United States."

"But they had our national insignia painted on them. That's what the news said. That's why our forces didn't shoot them down before they attacked."

"Even at Pearl Harbor, the Japanese flew planes with the rising sun on their wings," she said quietly.

"What?" I didn't understand her meaning then, but later I realized that she thought that it was a cowardly act to make people think the airplanes about to kill them were friendly ones.

The bombings were frightening enough, but two days later, on April 17, we learned that early in the morning a large rebel force had landed less than a three-hour journey south of Varadero along the Girón shore at a place known as the Bay of Pigs.

We were at war.

Marissa did not have to explain to me that the United States was behind it. Where had these insurgents gotten airplanes and landing craft and weapons if not from our hostile northern neighbor? And why were there U.S. warships patrolling dangerously close to Cuban waters?

"But why would a powerful country like the United States decide to fight a little country like ours?" I asked Marissa.

"They are afraid," she said.

"But what do they have to be afraid of?" It didn't make sense to me. We were only a small island in the Caribbean, and they were the most powerful nation in the world.

"It does seem ridiculous," she said. "But they are crazy afraid of Communism. Even of socialism. I think they are terrified that Fidel will join up with the Soviet Union to oppose them."

"I see," I said, but I really didn't see at all. Why would a country that fought to gain its own freedom oppose our effort to be free? And why would a nation with leaders like George Washington and

Abraham Lincoln, heroes whom we had studied about in school, want to support a terrible man like General Fulgencio Batista? Because they were afraid? Truly? It was hard for me to believe such a thing, even if Marissa did.

Our master teacher and many of the other leaders left immediately to go to the front. They had served in the revolutionary army, and they were ready to fight the invaders.

Before the day was over, parents began to arrive to demand that their children return home. My own father arrived just before bedtime. He had borrowed Ramón's car to get to Varadero. "You must come home," he said.

I had never before disobeyed my father. But I couldn't leave. I stood up as straight as I could and tried to smile. "Papi," I said, "I have signed on for the year. If I leave, it will be like a soldier deserting."

"You are not a soldier," he said. "You are a little girl."

"I am a member of the Conrado Benítez Brigade, and I am nearly fourteen," I said.

"Not until November," he said, correcting me. "You won't be fourteen for many months. And you will not have your quinceañera for another year and a half." He sighed, as though he knew the futility of that argument and tried another. "Oh, Lorita, you *promised* that if things got too bad . . ."

"But it's not bad at all here," I said. I had trouble looking into his face. It was too sad. "And certainly not too hard. I am learning how to be a teacher. My country needs me."

"We need you, Lora." He was almost whispering. "We need you to be safe at home. We lost Roberto to the revolution. We cannot lose you. You know it would break your mother's heart and send your beloved abuela to her grave."

I ached to see the sorrow and fear in his eyes, but even as I trembled inside, I remembered to stand up tall to show him I was determined. "If it gets too bad, too hard, I will come home, like I promised."

"That might be too late." He shook his head sadly. "The insurgents did not hesitate to kill Conrado Benítez." But my stiff spine must have convinced him that I would not give up, so he gently stroked my hair, kissed my cheek, and turned to go.

I called after him: "Give my love to everyone."

He looked back at me.

"I love you, Papi," I said.

"But you no longer obey me," he said softly. I watched him leave the room, and then I went to my bed and wet it with the tears of the child I still was.

The next morning, I said to Marissa, "I stood tall and tried to smile. At the moment it helped, but then after he left, all I could do was cry."

"Of course you cried," she said. "You love your papi."

CHAPTER SIX

Into the Escambray Mountains

APRIL 1961

While the battle raged on the southern beaches, we brigadistas were determined to continue on as though nothing had happened. Our group joined the class of one of the women master teachers. Our lessons went on as though nothing was more important than the war against illiteracy that we had sworn to fight. Of course, at mealtime, we gathered around to hear the latest news, but then we went back to work. We had joined an army, and we had to spend our time preparing for the campaign.

At first it seemed as if the invaders would triumph, but our military rallied. Only two days after the initial assault, the enemy began to flee to the boats that had brought them to our shore. And on April 20, the teachers who had left for the front returned to Varadero. The war was over. Many prisoners were taken, but a few, carrying their North American–made weapons with them, escaped into the mountains and joined the insurgents there. *No need to be afraid,* I told myself. If our militia could defeat an invading force backed by the powerful United States, they could surely protect us brigadistas from a few roving bandits. I told Marissa how glad I was that I hadn't gone home with Papi.

"No," she said. "Had you left, you would never have forgiven yourself for deserting the cause."

I will always remember the thrill of receiving my uniform and equipment. Dresses with frills and flouncy skirts were from my past life. Even the more severe pleated skirt and white blouse of my school days were left behind. Now I would wear the uniform of a brigadista. We were issued two khaki shirts and two pairs of trousers, a pair of sturdy boots with a change of socks, an olive-green beret, and a leather belt.

On our uniforms, we were to affix two badges, one large and one small, which I cherished. In the center of each badge was an open book upon which sat a large letter A and a pencil. In an arc above were the words THE ARMY OF LITERACY, and below our identification as CONRADO BENÍTEZ BRIGADE. There was a slot at the top of the large plastic badge, and our shirts had epaulettes, one end sewn to the shoulder and the other buttoned down. Marissa showed me how to thread the epaulette through the slot and then rebutton it to keep the badge secure. The small metal ones we pinned to the front of our shirts. Some people later moved theirs to their berets, which, I must confess, gave them a rather jaunty air. I wasn't quite bold enough to do that.

In addition to our uniforms, we were issued

our teachers' guide, our book of readings, copies of *Venceremos* and pencils for our students, and a rucksack for carrying our supplies. Each of us received a check for ten pesos for personal expenses—paper and stamps for writing home, toothpaste, soap—that sort of thing. We were not promised wages for our work—I had never expected to be paid—because we were a volunteer army. We were instructed to give our ration cards to our hosts, because they would be feeding us.

To my surprise, each of us was also issued a hammock and a huge lantern. "The campesinos will not have an extra bed for you," the master teacher explained. "Nor will they have any electricity. Classes will most likely be held after the workday is done. You will need a bright light to study under."

The day she was to leave for her assignment, Marissa sought me out. "I have something for you, Little One," she said. Then she took the necklace of Santa Juana seeds that always hung around her neck and hung them around mine. "I strung these myself," she said. "Wear them for good luck."

"But they're yours! You need them for yourself."

"I'll string myself another set when I get to the mountains." She patted the beads on my chest. "I don't want you to forget me."

"I could never forget you," I said, the tears starting in my eyes.

"Oh, shush," she said, wiping my cheek with her long fingers.

So while beneath my shirt I wore the rosary Abuela had given me when I made my first communion, over my shirt I always wore the necklace of Santa Juana seeds that had once belonged to Marissa. I was proud to wear those beads. Santa Juana, or Saint Joan, as she is known to English speakers, was a warrior saint, and the seeds from her namesake bush are thought to bring good fortune.

I thought I would not be able to get through my days at Varadero without Marissa, but I hardly had time to miss her, for two busy days later, I, too, was on my way. All of us who arrived on buses on the same day now piled into other buses and rode away. The bus I'd been loaded into drove south for about three hours, and then, because we were going into the mountains, we were transferred to large open trucks.

The thirty brigadistas who made up what was to become my squad were so crowded on the truck bed that at first we thought we couldn't sit down. But after the truck hit its first bump, we were all sprawled on top of one another. No one was hurt. We laughed and each person found a tiny spot to sit. We scrunched together on the rough plank flooring, so tightly packed that no matter how rough the road, we hardly swayed.

Perhaps all of us were afraid. I know I was. In fact, I was afraid that the persons on either side of me could feel my trembling. I had never been farther from home than the one-hour bus ride to Varadero. Now I was traveling into the Escambray Mountains — the truly unknown — except for one fact. It was in these mountains that Conrado Benítez had died.

Once we left the main highway and secondary roads, the way ahead became more of a track through the forest than a real road. I could see the trees looming over me when I craned my neck to look up, but that was all I could see of the forest from my place in the middle of the truck. Anyone or anything might be lurking in the shadows on either side.

Eventually the track became so narrow that heavy branches were brushing the side of the truck and the sun was blotted from view. Then someone began to sing the anthem of the campaign. I could feel my spirits lifting. In English, it won't sound anything like that wonderful song with which the mountains rang that day.

We are the Conrado Benítez Brigade;
We are the vanguard of the revolution.
With our books held high, we march to our goal,
To bring literacy to all of Cuba.

To the plains and the mountains we brigadistas
    will go,
Living with the people of the homeland,
Fighting for peace.

Down with imperialism; up with freedom!
Through the alphabet shines the light of truth.

For Cuba! Cuba!
Study, work, rifle!
Pencil, primer, manual!
With literacy! Literacy!
We shall prevail!

The first time I had heard the anthem, I was puzzled by the word *rifle*. I certainly never expected to carry a rifle. I had never even held a gun in my life, much less shot one. But Marissa explained to me that there were militias with rifles in the remote mountain areas. Fidel had promised our parents that the militia would protect the literacy brigade. And our men tried. But this is a big island, and there are many hiding places for those who would do evil.

CHAPTER SEVEN

Our Squad

BASE CAMP, APRIL 1961

The truck stopped where the track it had been following turned into a path. "Just wait here," the driver said as he pulled down the back to let us off. "Your squad leaders will be here soon."

Then he hopped up into the cab. He shouted for us to clear the way, and, with his head out of the window, backed rapidly down the narrow track and disappeared, leaving us standing there in the small forest clearing.

"Does anyone know where we're going?" one of the older boys asked. The rest of us shook our heads. "Then I guess there is nothing to do but wait."

At first it felt good to stand and move about after the long bumpy ride, but eventually we began to settle down. There was a fallen tree across the narrow path. The older girls claimed the log, and the older boys lounged against trees or found a rock to perch on. The rest of us put our rucksacks on the ground and sat on them. It was well past noon before we gave up straining our necks toward the path, looking for someone to appear. No one dared start a song. Who might be out there, just beyond earshot, in that dark forest?

We barely whispered to one another as we nibbled our lunch like rabbits. I suppose I should have been comforted by the knowledge that I wasn't alone in my fear, but I wasn't. I wanted the older ones to be brave. I wanted my comrades to say to me that there was nothing to be afraid of.

Across the narrow path, a lizard poked its head out from under a rock. It seemed to study us, and, satisfied that we were harmless, slid out and climbed the rock to a patch of sunlight on top. It sat with its head still and erect, but it curled and uncurled its little striped tail as though making the most of the warmth. I don't especially like reptiles, but that little curly-tailed lizard reminded me of home. They are everywhere — even in Havana. For a few minutes, it made those woods seem less alien.

"Shh," said Carlos, one of the older boys, even though we were being very quiet. He had seen someone coming down the path. "He has a gun."

We sat in frozen silence as an armed man came into view. And then we saw that he was being followed along the path by a young man and a young woman. They were both wearing the uniform and badges of the Conrado Benítez Brigade. We all began to laugh out of sheer nervous relief. The soldier was one of our own, protecting the pair who were to be our squad leaders, Esteban, our jefe, or commander, and Lilian, his assistant. We jumped to our feet, eager to follow them into our new life.

I don't think we hiked more than two or three kilometers before we came to a settlement of sorts.

Esteban told us this was our base. The thirty of us would be scattered about at various farms in the area, but on Sundays we were to return to base. "You will report your successes and your failures, and we will try to help one another become better teachers," he explained.

"And we'll have fun together, too," said Lilian. "It won't be all work."

I felt a little annoyed when she said that. I had come to work with the campesinos, not to play with other brigadistas.

The thirty of us, ten boys and twenty girls, were divided into neighborhood teams. Esteban carefully parceled out the boys so that each team would have one boy. Juan was the boy in my team, Maria the other girl.

I had watched Maria at lunch, while she sat on the log, eating her sandwich. I guess I always notice the pretty one. She had bright eyes; long, black, glossy hair; and the kind of skin my mother would have gushed over—she was the sort of girl the older boys would notice as well. I guessed she must be a couple of years older than I, and as it turned out she had recently turned sixteen.

Juan was shorter than I was, although he looked to be about my age. His cheeks were pimply, and he had a cockiness about him, but that might have just been to make up for his height. He seemed disappointed that the boys had been separated and that he would have two girls to work with. But he shook his head, as if to say, *Oh, well, it can't be helped,* and gave us a grin as he walked over to get acquainted.

When we were all standing about in our little teams, Esteban said, "Look carefully at these two people. Your team members will be the brigadistas you will know best and depend on most."

Esteban and Lilian began our orientation by sharing some of their own experiences. We knew they had been chosen to be our squad leaders because they had already proven themselves to be excellent teachers, so we listened as they reminded us that we must be respectful of our students, that we must write to our parents—and bring our letters on Sunday so that they could be posted—that we must take good care of the materials that we were given, and that we must keep a diary of our observations, our successes, and our failures.

"With so much that's new, it will be easy to forget important things," Lilian said. "You must write them down the day they happen."

And the same lessons we had been taught in Varadero were repeated in the mountains, step by step.

Step One: Conversation. Look at the photograph in the student book and find out what the students know about the picture. Encourage them to talk and or ask questions about the picture and figure out the meaning of the picture.

Step Two: The Reading. First, the teacher will slowly and clearly read the text beside the picture. Then the teacher and student will read the text together. Finally the student will read the text alone.

Step Three: Practice and Exercise. Seek recognition of a phrase or sentence. Break up each phrase or sentence into syllables. Examine each syllable within an exercise.

The first image in the primer was a picture of a number of men in suits and dark ties conferring together. And the word to be learned was OEA, which is not a word at all but three vowels that in Spanish stand for the Organización de los Estados Americanos, or as it's known in English, the OAS, the Organization of American States. When I first saw that page in Varadero, I wondered what those initials would mean to a poor farmer in a remote mountainous area of Cuba, but once the master teacher explained it, it seemed quite obvious.

After our successful revolution, the United States began to put pressure on the governments in the OEA (or OAS) that had been allies of our former dictator to oppose our new government. We needed the campesinos in the remote areas to understand that because of this situation, we were unable to import many needed goods, including medicine, tools, and machinery, even trucks and tractors. These outsiders were determined to ensure that our revolution would fail, so that the old order could return in triumph.

The initials OEA, our teacher said, were a good way not only to convey a political lesson, but also to introduce three vowels to people who had never heard either of the OEA or the concept of a vowel. So, ironically, our enemies proved a great help to the literacy campaign, without even knowing it.

Step-by-step, students then would move from learning vowels and consonants to learning words, short phrases, then sentences. At the same time, the lessons would help our students understand about our country after the revolution—about land reform, cooperative stores, the conversion of buildings that once belonged to the rich into homes and schools for the poor.

But our primary goal was literacy. Our leaders knew, and we knew, that in order to become a strong nation, we needed strong citizens. And to be a responsible citizen, you must know how to read and write.

We learned a lot in those three days. Although I never got to know Juan as well as Esteban had predicted, my friendship with Maria began that first night at base camp. In the late afternoon, Esteban gave us hooks and told us to find a place to hang our hammocks outdoors. There wouldn't be room for thirty of us to sleep in the small houses surrounding the clearing.

"C'mon," said Maria. "There aren't that many good places, but I scouted out a spot earlier, and if we hurry, we can grab it." Maria's place was at the edge of the woods. Two giant ceiba trees stood side by side, about a hammock's distance apart. There were no blossoms yet. It was too early, but the foliage, even the thorns, was magnificent.

"Perfect, don't you think?"

"Perfect for one hammock," I said. "As long as you avoid the thorns."

"No worries. I'll make it work. You hand me the hooks." She found a safe spot and screwed a hook into one of the ceiba trees. Then I handed her a second hook and she screwed that in the other ceiba. "Now, give me your hammock."

I unbuckled my rucksack and took out the books on top to dig down into the bag to get my hammock.

She watched me, clearly amused. "Loaded down with books, I see."

I blushed. "I couldn't live without something to read," I said.

"Well, you're the one who has to carry the extra weight. Here, give me that."

I handed her my hammock, which she quickly stretched between the two trees.

"But what about you?" I asked.

"Don't worry," she said. She took a third hook and screwed it into a nearby pine. Then she hung one end of her own hammock on the same hook holding one end of my hammock and stretched the other end to the hook on the pine tree. "See?" she said. "Nice and cozy."

Although we had been squashed tighter than peas in a pod in the truck, our rucksacks and lanterns poking each other, sometimes painfully, it was that first night at base camp that we really became a squad. Esteban and two of the other boys had made a fire in the center of the tiny village. We gathered there after dark, and Lilian asked us each to introduce ourselves—where we were from and what we hoped would happen this year while we were brigadistas.

I didn't learn too much about my comrades through those self-introductions. All of us were students. Most of our parents had been reluctant to let us join. All of us wanted to know at the end of the year that we had successfully carried out our mission.

But Juan said he hoped to be eighteen centimeters taller by December. And Isora's story was the big surprise. She was only twelve—the only person in our squad younger than I.

"My papi signed for my sister Adria, who is fifteen," Isora said, "but he wouldn't sign for me, no matter how much I begged. So, what could I do? I copied his signature from Adria's permission. It was perfect. I'm a good writer. And Adria would never tell." She giggled. "Adria sneaked my bag on the bus for me, and Papi didn't know what had happened until he saw me waving good-bye from the bus window."

Everyone, including me, clapped, but I really didn't know if I was impressed or horrified.

Carlos had a guitar, and after the introductions, we started to sing songs we all knew by heart. At first Carlos played comic songs of the street, but as the embers began to die, the songs grew more melancholy — songs of lost love and far-away home. It was hard to sing past the lump in my throat. "I miss the sea already," he said, and sang a song I'd never heard of stars above the water.

We were all quiet for a long time and then Lilian said, "Look at the stars."

I bent my head back to look up. I thought I'd seen stars before, but it had always been in the city, with all its lights. And in Varadero we'd been in our dorms soon after dark. So I drank in the sight that first night in the country. Where there are no lights, and even the moon is hidden, the sky is like a bucket of diamonds thrown across black velvet.

Later as we lay in our hammocks, our toes close to our shared hook, Maria told me how much she had hoped we would be teamed with Enrico. "You know who he is," she said. "He's the good-looking one. With the beautiful smile."

Enrico was tall and quite dark—admittedly the handsomest one of the four older boys. He did have very white teeth and a lovely smile. "He's nice looking," I said.

"Nice looking? He's fantastic," she said. "Which one do you like?"

"Oh, I don't know. I'm really not old enough to be thinking about boys."

"Pooh. I bet your mother told you that."

I blushed in the dark, because I did know which one I liked—Carlos. I loved his playing and his singing. He had the heart of a poet. I was sure of it.

"No boyfriends, eh? Just books. So, what are all those books of yours about?"

"Only three," I said. "I just brought three books."

"Well, what are they about?"

"One is a collection of poems by José Martí. The fat one is an English novel. I need to work on my English while I'm here."

"And the other?"

"I had to bring my English-Spanish dictionary so I could look up words in the novel."

"Oh," she said. "You must be quite the scholar." I wondered if she thought I was trying to show off. I hoped I didn't seem to be one of those snooty intellectuals my mother had been afraid I would become.

"What's your novel about?"

"It's—well, I guess it's a kind of a love story."

"A romance novel?"

"I never really thought of it that way, but . . ."

"North American?"

"No, English. It's set in the early nineteenth century, so—"

"Really old-fashioned European stuff, then."

"It doesn't feel so old-fashioned."

"And Martí? You like him?"

"Don't you?"

"I don't know. I guess everybody's supposed to, but I could never really get into him. The teachers were always telling us what everything meant—everything he ever said. I got a little tired of it."

If I had hoped Maria would be another Norma, I realized quickly this would not be the case. Nor would she be a wise and sisterly Marissa. She turned out to be just Maria, and, in the end, that was enough.

I never even tried to talk to Juan about literature. He and the other young boys seemed to think about nothing but war and politics.

The three nights we were together at base camp, we ended every evening with Carlos leading us in song. The next two nights we danced as well. On the final night, the nearby campesinos emptied their houses and joined us — even the little children, who should have been long asleep. They taught us a dance of the mountains that none of us had ever seen before, and Maria and little Isora, who had television sets at home, taught everyone the Twist, which was the newest craze from North America. It seemed strange to be dancing like our enemies, but I have to admit it was fun. Even solemn Esteban was twisting with delight. "I don't care if it did come from them," he said. "It's better than bombs."

CHAPTER EIGHT

My New Family

ARRIVING ON ASSIGNMENT, EARLY MAY 1961

It was time to leave the base camp and go to our new homes. Even if there were still jumping beans in my stomach, I felt reasonably prepared, and I truly wanted to start my assignment. The three of us — Juan, Maria, and I — were going to an area not much more than a half hour's walk from base. Lilian took Juan to his place, but Esteban felt it was important for him to introduce us girls. I suppose he wanted to indicate to any reluctant men that he, as a man, had approved us to be teachers of men.

We stopped first at Maria's farm. Everyone rushed from the house or from across the field to welcome her with open arms. They were so excited, they said. They had hardly been able to wait for their very own teacher. Maria, in turn, was almost jumping up and down as she expressed her own pleasure that she had been permitted to come to their home and be with them. She just knew it was going to be a wonderful time all around for everyone.

I watched her and, I must say, I was impressed. She didn't seem a bit anxious. In fact, she acted so happy that I felt a pang of envy watching her. Any feeling of superiority I might have developed at base camp melted on the spot. Maria wasn't going to have any trouble relating to illiterate campesinos. She was practically a member of the family already— long before she had even opened the primer to page one. At any rate, I would soon realize that I had been so preoccupied with watching her interact with her new family I had not even looked at the house she was going to live in. If I had, the first look at my own new home might not have been such a shock.

I hope I was able to conceal my dismay as we approached the house where I was to stay. It was a two-room shack, not a proper house at all. The walls were built of rough planks with palm thatch for a roof. At least there was a real door and not just palm branches across the entrance.

The farmer was out in the field, but he spotted us coming through the trees. He came to us, carrying his hoe, and spoke a quiet greeting to Esteban, whom he seemed to know, then smiled shyly at me. Esteban told him my name. He told me his—Luis Santana—and started to extend his hand but realized how dirty it was and simply wiped it on his pant leg.

"Welcome," he said formally, and walked hurriedly away to the house. I supposed he was telling the rest of his family that we had arrived. Esteban and I waited outside the door. It may have been a few minutes. It seemed like hours. We could hear some talking inside, but not what was being said. There were the high-pitched voices of little children, objecting, as I imagined, to having their faces washed before they met the strange visitor. I smiled at Esteban, trying not to show how anxious I was, but he sensed it and patted my shoulder.

The family finally straggled out of the door, following their father, who now offered me a clean hand and repeated his name. Then he stepped aside and presented his wife, whom he called Veronica. The three children were tiny, so I guessed that Luis and Veronica were perhaps younger than they looked. Their faces were as dark and leathery as dried tobacco, and their hands, when they shook mine, were very rough. The little boy stood stiffly beside his father, and the even smaller girls hid behind their mother.

"You must meet the teacher," Luis said. "Tell her your names."

The boy whispered something and then the little girls did as well, but their hands were covering their faces, so I had no idea what any of them had said. I knelt down close to them. "Excuse me," I said. "I didn't hear your names." The boy looked at his father for help while the tiny girls giggled behind their hands.

"My son, Rafael, is six. My daughters are Emilia, who is five, and little Isabel, who has just turned three," their father said.

"You have beautiful children," I said. The tiny smiles on the parents' faces told me that I had said the right thing.

When Luis ushered us all inside, I could see that the floor was just dirt, but swept clean. In the back room, there were two straw mattresses on the floor. The farmer and his wife apparently slept on one and the three children on the other. There was no mattress for me, or even room for another mattress. After much discussion, they decided that the teacher should hang her hammock across a corner of the kitchen. However, I would have to take it down each morning, or there would be no way to reach the dishes and stored foodstuffs. A table and stools stood in the center of the kitchen. Esteban asked the farmer for rope so that he could hang my lantern on a beam over the table. "The government wants to be sure you have plenty of light to study by," he explained.

I didn't say much that evening. None of us did. The children stared at me over their plates of stew, which consisted of beans and a mixture of vegetables over rice. There was no meat that night, but I found the food very tasty. When I complimented Veronica on it, she ducked her head and blushed.

It was nearly dark by the time the meal was finished, but there was no mention of lighting the government lantern. The family simply retired to the back room, and I hung my hammock on the hooks Luis had provided and climbed in.

I had slept in the hammock at base camp, but Maria and some of the other girls were close by. I'd never felt alone. But that first night at the Santanas', it felt unbearably lonely to be lying there in the dark by myself. It is so dark in the country. In Havana it is never totally dark, but there wasn't even a moon that night, and once the sun set, it was blacker than black in that tiny room from which I could not see the stars. The blackness seemed to enhance the noises of the night—the stirring of the family on their straw mattresses, a sleepy murmur from one of the children, a low grunt from one of the pigs, the rustle of one of the large animals, restless in the stockade, and then, a sound I could not identify from farther off in the woods. A lonely, lonely cry. *It's only a bird, I told myself, just a bird.*

I longed for my family—for my mother fussing over me if she heard me cough in the night, for Abuela's quiet snoring, for simply knowing that beyond my closed eyelids the lights of my city were coming through my window and the noises I heard were that of the occasional car driving past my home.

Only that morning, even as late as that very afternoon, I had felt prepared, eager to start my new life as a teacher. Now the truth was like a stone lying on my chest. I knew at last why my parents had been so afraid for me. I *was* too young. I had had no experience to speak of as a person, much less as a teacher. And the people I would be living with seemed so timid around me. I wanted so much for them to like me. Maria had made an instant warm connection with her family, and I didn't have any idea how she had done it. I was not good at making friends — look how few I had made at school! Only Norma, and she was more of an outcast than I was. There was Marissa, but she had probably befriended me when I arrived at Varadero because she felt sorry for me.

I lay awake long into the night, wondering why I had volunteered, why I'd been accepted, why anyone had ever imagined that I was up to the challenge. Finally, I forced myself to turn my thoughts away from my fears and toward the family in the next room. Even if they didn't like me, they had asked for a teacher and volunteered to take one into their home, so they must want to learn — they must want to be able to read and write. And like it or not, I was the person that had been sent to them. But was I up to the task of teaching them? At that moment I could hardly believe that I was.

It felt as though I had barely gotten to sleep in my swaying bed when a rooster began to crow. I rolled out of the hammock and pulled on my uniform as quickly as I could in the semidarkness, hoping to be decent before anyone came in to fix breakfast. I was taking down my hammock when Veronica slipped into the room. "Buenos días, Maestra," she said softly. She had called me "teacher," even though I had taught her nothing yet.

"Buenos días, Veronica," I said, and quickly added, "Please call me Lora."

She smiled and nodded, but many months would pass before she ever called me by my name.

That morning our team began our work. The first task for Juan and Maria and me was the census. That meant that we went from house to house on the neighboring farms to discover who was literate and who was not. Between houses, Maria wanted to discuss Enrico. *Didn't I think he was handsome? And so intelligent!*

"You girls think only of boys," Juan said. "We are here to do a job, not gossip about boys!"

I wanted to protest. *I* was here to do a job. Had

he heard me say a word about boys? Maybe he was just jealous because none of the girls were making eyes at him, as short and scrawny as he was, with a face blossoming in pimples. But to my relief, his admonition stopped Maria's mooning for the time being, and we went on with our canvas.

When we came to my own house, we learned that neither Luis nor Veronica had ever been to school. There wasn't a school for miles, and even as tiny children, they had worked on the farm. They both ducked their heads in shame when they spoke of their ignorance. Luis wouldn't meet my eyes when he said, "I want you to teach me how to write my name. Then I will no longer have to mark an X or press my thumb to the paper when I vote or sign some important document. That is the most important thing. If, before the year is over, I can write *Luis Santana,* I will be satisfied."

Our closest neighbors were the Acosta family, an old man and woman and their son and new daughter-in-law. The women were eager to learn, but the old man shook his balding head while his son glared with disdain. Daniel, the young man, told me bluntly, "My father and I do not want to take lessons from a little girl, and our wives are too busy to spend time with this nonsense."

The women looked stricken.

"That is why the lessons will be at night, when the work day is over," Maria said. "During the day, we brigadistas will work side by side with you."

"What do you children from the cities know about our life? Nothing! You will only be in the way."

I finally mustered up the courage to speak. "You are right," I said. "We know nothing about the hard work you and your wives must do. But we're here to learn as well as to share what we know."

Nancy, his new wife, stepped forward. "Please sign me up for the lessons. And my mother-in-law as well. We talked to Lilian last week about the campaign. We want to learn."

Her husband didn't even look at her. "No one from this house will be going to Santana's house for lessons. Now—we have work to do." And he turned on his heel and went into the farmhouse.

* * *

We divided the potential students among the three of us. I was assigned only to Luis and Veronica. The Acostas should have been part of my class, but it didn't look as though any of them would be coming.

"Be patient," Lilian said the following Sunday when I told her how I'd failed to register them. "Those men are stubborn, but their women may win them over if you cannot."

CHAPTER NINE

Writing His Own Name

The next morning, I was up again before Veronica came into the kitchen. "You should sleep longer, Maestra," she said, even though that would have been difficult since my hammock took up so much of the kitchen.

"No," I said. "I want to do everything with you. That is as much my job as teaching is."

She smiled her shy smile. "Then our first job is to fetch the water."

She picked up two large metal cans and carried them out the door. I followed her to the crude stockade that surrounded the oxen and goats. She hitched a wagon to the ox team and loaded on the empty containers. They were large and filled the small wagon. "This way," she said. "We must go to the river."

I walked beside Veronica as she guided the oxen. She was a tiny woman, but the oxen were totally under her control. "How did you learn to drive them?" I asked.

She laughed. "These two? They are as gentle as pet rabbits. Here—" She made as if to hand me the reins. "You try."

"No, no. Not today. They don't know me yet. Maybe later."

It was a beautiful spring morning. The orchids and hibiscus and flowers whose names I'll never know painted the way with brilliant color. The birds were singing. I felt a bit as Eve might have felt her first morning in Eden. That is, until Veronica noticed my enchanted gaze and said a bit sharply, "We must watch the path for snakes. They won't kill you, but the bite will hurt." I was glad to be wearing my boots.

I learned a lot that day—how to fill the large cans with water from the river (Veronica hefted her heavy can with ease—it was weeks before I stopped sweating and grunting), how to boil coffee, how to wash clothes on the rocks by the river (if only my mother could have seen me!), how to feed the chickens and the goats and the oxen, how to prepare a meal. In time, I would even learn to skillfully milk a goat (that took a while, believe me), cut corn with a machete, ride a horse (granted, an old, slow one), and plow a field behind a team of oxen (not that my furrows were ever straight). My skin would turn brown, and my hands become calloused.

But during those early weeks, I longed for thick gloves to protect my skin. Cornstalks are rough, and the worms on the tomatoes and tobacco were squishy, and, well, I was a bit squeamish in those days. I tried to remind myself that many of my fellow brigadistas were working on sugar plantations where cutting cane is ruinous for one's hands. Others had been sent to enormous tobacco estates with thousands of plants, not just the small patch Luis cultivated for the bit of cash the leaves might bring in. If every muscle in my body protested after a day hoeing corn or digging up yams, just how would I have managed on an estate of hundreds of acres? Or such was the lecture I'd give myself as I tried to straighten my aching back after an hour or two bent over a row of beans.

"Take a rest, Lora," Luis would say. But pride would keep me at a task until it was done. To my amusement, he began holding me up as an example to Emilia. "See, Emilia? Aren't you ashamed, running off to play when there is still work to be done? Lora hasn't stopped working." I didn't remind her father that Emilia, after all, was only five.

But I am getting ahead of the story. That night Luis, Veronica, and I sat at the kitchen table under our bright lantern and began the first lesson in the primer. Because Luis was so eager to learn how to write his name, I wrote both their names in large chalk letters on the piece of slate Veronica had put up for a blackboard. The first lesson, you may remember, was to learn the vowels *o, e,* and *a.* I pointed out the *a*'s in *Santana* and *Veronica.* "And soon we will do the other vowels, *i* and *u,* which are in *Luis,*" I promised.

I didn't realize that one of the first lessons would have to be how to hold a pencil. Veronica watched me carefully as I wrote the initial letters, OEA, but Luis eagerly grabbed up his pencil and clutched it in his fist as though it were an ax poised to chop up his workbook.

"Today," I said, "Veronica had to teach me how to light the stove so I wouldn't set the house on fire. Tonight, please let me show you the best way to hold a pencil so both the pencil and the workbook will survive your attack on the alphabet."

Luis looked up, puzzled. But when he realized I was joking, he laughed and let go of his tight grip on the pencil. Then he allowed me to demonstrate a more gentle and effective method of wielding his new tool.

Lessons were erased daily from the slate, but never their names, which Luis always looked at longingly night by night until, after he knew his vowels and consonants — indeed all the alphabet — I wrote his name in his workbook and suggested he practice copying it. Then came the night I erased his name from the slate and urged him to try his hand at writing it where I had written it two weeks before.

The chalk was tight in his hand and his tongue peeked out the corner of his mouth, as painstakingly he wrote, for the first time, his own name for others to see. At the final *a,* he let out something between a gasp and a laugh.

"You did it," I said. "You wrote *Luis Santana.*"

"I wrote my name," he said, "and my wife and my teacher can both read it, right? My name. Luis Santana. Now everyone who can read will know that I am Luis Santana."

"Wait, let me get my camera." I fetched my uncle Roberto's camera from my rucksack. "Now stand there — no, don't hide your signature. Stand a little to your left so I can see both your smile and your name."

I've taken many photos since, but none I treasure more.

In the midst of our celebration, there was a call from outside the door. We turned to see who could be visiting at this time of night. At some point during those first busy days, I had forgotten to be afraid of marauding insurgents, but I felt a chill at the call. Luis went to the door. It was the Acostas—all four of them. "We have brought the women for the lessons," Daniel said gruffly.

"Everyone come in," Luis said. "Everyone must see." He made no attempt to contain his pride. "You must look here," he said, pointing at his signature on the slate. "I can write my name."

"How wonderful!" Nancy exclaimed. "Now you can sign your name and not just your thumbprint."

"How do you know it means anything?" her husband said grumpily. "It's just scribbling."

"No," said Luis. "It's real writing. I know

because I can read it. Look here—*L-u-i-s*, Luis, and *S-a-n-t-a-n-a*, Santana. Luis Santana. That is my name in letters, so that anyone who can read will be able to tell what it is."

"I can read it," said Veronica softly. "*Veronica* is longer and harder, so . . ."

"But you're practicing," I said. "Soon you'll be able to write it on the slate for everyone to read."

"Did we come too late for the lesson?" Nancy asked.

"No," I said. "If Luis and Veronica don't mind a review, I can start the first lesson with you and your mother tonight."

"You and Joaquin should join," Luis said to Daniel. "Lora is a good teacher."

Daniel made a sound like *humf.* "We'll wait outside for the women," he said, and then turned to his wife. "But don't you be long. We have work to do tomorrow."

It went that way for several nights. The Acosta men sat on the ground outside the door while their womenfolk studied under the lantern. Nancy was very bright and quickly caught up with Luis and Veronica. Her mother-in-law, Dunia, despite her determination, was having trouble making out any words.

One afternoon, Veronica suggested that I leave the washing for her to finish and go and give Dunia a private lesson. I hesitated, but she urged me to help her neighbor, and so I went.

"Do you know why my son relented and let Nancy and me join the lessons?" Dunia asked me that afternoon.

"No, but I'm very glad he did."

She laughed. "I live with two stubborn men, but Nancy knows how to handle them. When Daniel refused to let her go to the lessons, she packed her clothes and went home to her mother's house. When Daniel went to bring her home, she said she would not return unless he allowed the two of us to come to your class. She was not going to give her child two ignorant parents. You see, she will be having Daniel's first child in November, and the thought that his child would not be born in his own home was too much for my son to bear, so he agreed." She snorted. "Macho men. If only I had been as clever as my daughter-in-law when I was a young bride."

It was also at that private lesson that I realized that Dunia had trouble reading because, although she could often make out the words I wrote up on the slate, the small letters in the workbook were for her simply blurs on the page.

When I told Lilian the next Sunday about the problem, she said, "The eye doctor will be coming to our area soon. Señora Acosta should get an examination."

When the doctor came, Joaquin accompanied his wife to the examination, and it turned out they both needed glasses. Oh, how proud they were of their new government-issued glasses.

"I can see a bird in that tree!" Dunia cried.

"*Humf,*" said Joaquin. "I can see a mosquito."

By the next night, we had three Acostas with us at the table.

Daniel hung around outside the door, but he

was secretly listening to the activity inside. Finally, I think he realized that if he didn't have his own pencil and workbook, he would never be able to write his name like the rest of his family—and how embarrassing would that be? Everyone, including his wife and his old mother, able to sign their names, while he would have to put his thumb on the ink pad and make a print? That wouldn't do at all.

I loved detailing these triumphs in my diary. Each week, I could hardly wait for Sunday to come so I could share my students' progress with the rest of the squad. Since Maria and I were the closest neighbors, I would go by her house and we would go together to our meetings at the base camp. I didn't try to share my life with her on the way because she was too full of talk about Enrico, how he was paying her special attention. I enjoyed being in on her romance, but, actually, I had never seen Enrico speak to Maria beyond a casual hello. When I ventured to say so, she assured me that was because he was not only dedicated to his work but adorably shy.

"Bring your camera next week," she said. "I know

if I ask him to have his picture taken with me, he'll jump at the chance." I wasn't so sure, but I brought my camera anyhow. I only had a few shots left, and I wanted to send off the roll of film with Esteban when he made his next trip into Gavilanes, which was our nearest town. I was eager to share the pictures of my farm family with my family in Havana.

I asked Esteban to make sure they gave me two copies of every print. I needed to give Luis a picture of himself standing beside his name.

As much as I grew to love my family and the Acostas, our Sunday gatherings at the base camp were a treat. Esteban didn't want us walking through the forest after dark, so he insisted we start home long before sundown. There were no songs around the fire. But we still had music. Carlos brought his guitar every Sunday, and Lilian was not above cutting off an Esteban lecture in midsentence to announce that it was time for a break.

Carlos always played cheerful songs, and Maria and Isora would jump up to start the dancing. At first, I just watched. Dancing in the firelight during those first nights at base camp had been one thing, but now I was a bit shy about dancing in the bright daylight. Everyone seemed to be a better dancer than I was. But Maria wouldn't let me sit there watching for long. She pulled me to my feet. "You must dance," she said. So I did. And a minute later, Carlos shouted across to me, "That's more like it, Lorita!" I'm sure my face turned the color of a ripe strawberry, but, of course, I was thrilled. It felt so good to be a part of a crowd of friends and not a lonely someone looking in longingly from the outside.

CHAPTER TEN

I Can Read!

ON ASSIGNMENT, JUNE–JULY 1961

I began to spend a day each week working at the Acostas'. They didn't need me as much as the Santanas, as they had four capable adults to do the chores, whereas at my house there were only two. But Luis felt strongly that I should spend some daylight time with the neighbors. He was right, of course. Chopping corn together, we got to know each other better, and though Daniel never really apologized for his earlier rudeness to me, he made a real effort to listen carefully during the lessons and work hard.

The Acostas were always glad to see me when I came to their farm, and it eased the initial awkwardness of their studying with me. One day Daniel and I had a race to see who could fill a basket of beans first.

"You lose!" he crowed.

"No fair," I said. "Your arms are longer."

"What do long arms have to do with it? It's skill."

"Well. You've been picking longer—years longer."

"Can I help it if all you've done is read books?"

I had to laugh. Not because anything was so terribly funny, but because sour-faced Daniel and I were actually having fun together.

One day he had fetched the Santanas' oxen for plowing, as the two families shared their use. When it was time for me to go home, Daniel asked me to drive the pair home and save him the round-trip. I was very honored that he would trust me with this errand.

Having all four Acostas in the class made

everything more lively. However, teaching Joaquin how to write his name became something of a challenge. He looked at what I had written on the slate and said, "That's not my name."

"Yes, it is," I said. "*J-o-a-q-u-i-n*. That is the way to spell *Joaquin*."

"No," he protested. "It should be *J-o-a-c-i-n*. You taught us *ca, ce, ci, co, cu*. It should be *ci*, like you taught us."

"No, Joaquin, I'm sorry. I didn't teach you that. I told you it's *ca, co, cu*, but the *c* before *i* and *e* is pronounced like an *s* sound. *C-i* is pronounced 'si.' You wouldn't want to pronounce Joaquin 'Joasin,' would you? Of course not. So the proper spelling of your name is *J-o-a-q-u-i-n*."

"Why?"

"I don't know why," I said. "I didn't decide it. Maybe somebody long ago in Spain decided on this funny way to write it. It's strange, but that's the way it is. And if you want someone to look at what you've written and read 'Joaquin,' this is the way you will have to spell it."

He shook his head. "It makes no sense," he grumbled.

"No, it doesn't, and I'm sorry, but there's nothing I can do about it. It's just the way it is."

"When I write my letter, I will tell Fidel it is wrong and tell him to change it. We won our freedom from Spain many years ago. Those stupid imperialists have no right to tell us how to write our own names."

On Sunday when I read this story aloud from my diary, all my friends laughed with delight. "He's perfectly right," Lilian said. "You must encourage Joaquin to write Fidel and tell him so."

Writing a letter to Fidel was not a joke. It was part of the final exam for those who had completed the primer. There were three tests. The first test required students to write their full names and addresses. Then they were required to read and write six simple words, three simple sentences, and a short paragraph. For the intermediate test, the words and sentences to be read were harder. The final test consisted of a paragraph with quite difficult words. In

English it went something like: "The revolutionary government wants to turn Cuba into an industrialized society. Many industries will be started. Many people will have jobs. There will be no more unemployment."

After the paragraph was read, the student was required to write out answers to several questions related to the paragraph. Then he or she had to turn the paper over and write out the paragraph as the teacher dictated it.

Finally, the student was to write a letter to Dr. Fidel Castro. When our leader announced the literacy campaign, he said that he wanted every student who completed the primer to write him a letter. So the letter became part of the final test.

Every night I looked at my students, their heads bent over their workbooks, the bright light of the lantern shining on their hair, and wondered if any of them would pass the final test before the end of the year. Was it an impossible goal? They were trying so hard. We were all trying so hard, and they could all, at last, write their own names, but it was the middle of the summer before my best students, Luis and Nancy, passed the first test.

For all her seeming giddiness about love, Maria must have been a good teacher. All six of her students had passed their first tests and were well on their way to taking the second. My envy of her looks and warm personality gave way to my envy of her success. But she never lorded it over me.

"I'm just lucky. My students are all so eager," she said. "They are easy to teach."

In the midst of my discouragement, there were wonderful moments. I remember when it was old Dunia's turn to read a paragraph. She pushed her glasses back up on the bridge of her nose and, with a finger on each word, she struggled through the two-sentence paragraph. Then she went back to the beginning and read the paragraph again. Then a third time, the pitch of her voice going up with excitement as she tore through the short passage. She raised her head, her eyes wide behind the thick lenses. "I can read!" she cried out. "I can read!"

"Yes," I said. "You can read. You have been reading for quite some time, but you didn't realize it."

Everyone began to laugh and clap. I may have
been the only one with tears in my eyes. *I must write
home about this,* I thought. My parents must be told
how wonderful it is to witness such ecstasy and to
know that you have played a part in creating it. And,
of course, I could hardly wait until Sunday to tell
Esteban and Lilian and the rest of the squad about
my triumph.

CHAPTER ELEVEN

Danger

JULY 1961

Some weeks after the Acostas had joined our class, Joaquin offered the use of their horse, Bonita, for Maria and me to ride to our Sunday meetings with our advisers. Neither of us had ever ridden a horse before, but the Acostas' old mare was as gentle as Joaquin had promised — and slow, really slow. We might have gotten there faster on our own two feet, but we couldn't risk hurting Joaquin's feelings. He seemed so proud to have something to offer the teachers. Besides, horseback riding was one more thing to add to the long list of things I was learning in the mountains.

That particular Sunday morning, I was especially impatient as I waited outside Maria's house, bursting as I was to tell everyone about Dunia's triumphant accomplishment. But for Maria, Sunday was the day she would see Enrico, so, as usual, she was spending a long time brushing her hair and primping. If either of us had owned any makeup, I'm not sure if we'd have gotten to the weekly meetings before noon.

One look at the alarmed faces awaiting our arrival, and my high spirits crashed to the ground before we had even dismounted. "What's the matter?" I asked.

For a moment, each one waited for someone else to speak. Then Lilian said softly, "Tie up the horse and come inside. We need to talk."

I did as she directed and followed the advisers and the other latecomers into the largest house in the village. We squeezed into the front room, which was already jammed with uniformed bodies. About half of the squad had spilled over into the adjoining room. The few kitchen stools were pushed under the table. No one was attempting to sit down. No one was making a sound.

"The militia was here last night," Esteban said quietly. "Yesterday they came upon a campsite, obviously one belonging to the counterrevolutionaries. They were able to track down and surround a dozen or so of the bandidos in the hills about ten kilometers from here. But they are sure some of them escaped. Those captured boasted that others would come and kill all the literacy teachers in the area."

My heart jumped in my chest. I am truly not a brave person.

"Well, that's good they were captured," said Juan. "But what will they do with prisoners? There're no jails around here."

"They have taken no prisoners," said Lilian softly.

"Oh," said Juan.

"But there are still live insurgents out there," said Esteban, trying to change the subject for those of us imagining yesterday's brutal scene. "You are to be careful. Maybe stay inside your houses for a few days, just until the militia finds the runaways."

"But I'm plowing tomorrow!"

"I have to hoe the corn!"

"I'm doing the washing," I said quietly. Everyone looked at me. They knew that washing had to be done at the riverside, not in a field close to the house.

Esteban shook his head. "Do what you must," he said. "But do be careful. Don't wear your uniforms outside your houses. There will be no more Sunday meetings until the militia tells us it is safe to move about the area."

I can remember how quiet I was on the way to Maria's house. She kept up a nervous chatter about Enrico. How charming and brave and wonderful he was.

"The picture you took for me? I'm sending it to my parents. I want them to see the beautiful man I am going to marry."

"Marry? Who? What?"

"Enrico! You weren't listening to me."

"I'm sorry," I said. And I was. I hadn't been listening. "What were you saying?"

This time she repeated, with a trace of impatience in her voice, that she was sending the picture I had taken to show her parents the man she was planning to marry.

I was startled. I had written off all her carrying on as a teenage crush. Nothing more. Finally I said, "Do you really think you're in love with him?"

"Oh, yes, yes," she said. "And I know he's in love with me."

"Really?" I couldn't imagine when they had ever been alone together. We always did everything in the big group. How could either of them be sure of anything?

"Oh, yes," she said. "It's true. I know he loves me. His eyes have told me so."

I could picture Enrico's dark eyes shining out of his very dark skin. He *was* quite beautiful, but he smiled at everyone, not just Maria.

"He was very happy when I showed him the picture of us you took."

"Really?" I was beginning to sound like a broken record, but I didn't want my friend to be hurt. Her idea of Enrico's love seemed to me more like a fantasy spun out of wishful thinking than reality. Reality was live insurgents roaming the forest — and dead ones lying in the bush.

It was not until I had dropped Maria off and was on the way home that I realized that I hadn't told anyone about Dunia's triumph. What kind of brigadista was I — thinking only of my own safety and not of my students?

I didn't say anything to Luis and Veronica about what had gone on at the meeting. I didn't want my fear to spread like a contagion to my farm families, because by now, they *were* my family. But they knew, somehow, about the new danger. That night when it was time for class, Luis said, "We must move our studies to the back room."

"There's no table in there," I said.

He lit the lamp in the kitchen. "Show her," he said to Veronica.

"Come with me, Maestra," Veronica said, taking

my hand and leading me out of the house. We went across the fields and into the trees beyond. "Do you see?"

From far away, even through the foliage, I could see the brilliant light of our lantern hanging from the rafter, and beneath it, the form of a man and the heads of two children bobbing about inside. "You see? A man with a powerful gun could shoot anyone from this distance," she said.

I shivered at the thought.

To my surprise, the Acostas came that night. They did not question the move. We sat on the mattresses next to the sleeping little girls, and the students wrote on their laps. It was awkward, but no one complained.

CHAPTER TWELVE

Life Goes On

ON ASSIGNMENT, JULY–SEPTEMBER 1961

I wrote my own family in Havana every week, but mail was seldom delivered into the mountains, so I had received only one letter from home since I'd left Varadero on April 28. My one letter came from my mother after I'd been in the mountains about three weeks, asking me how I was, what sort of toilet facilities were available, in short, if life in the country was too hard for me.

So you can imagine that I never included in my own letters any fears or frustrations I might have.

Yes, I said, life was different, it took getting used to, but it was a challenge, and they all knew how much I loved a challenge. (I stopped writing when I wrote that sentence. Should I erase the part about their knowing I loved a challenge? Did any of my family think I loved a challenge? Well, I did like to study hard subjects. And I had dared to join the campaign. Surely they would recognize those as challenges. I left it in.) I was learning so much, I said. Could they believe that I could milk a goat? Boil coffee? Wash clothes on a rock? Cut corn with a machete?

And the Santana children were darling. Luis and Veronica were like an older brother and sister to me, etc., etc., etc. I was simply a fountain of cheer. In my weekly letters home, that is. But this week, I wasn't sure what I could write after Esteban's grim warnings.

The next morning after breakfast, I took off my beloved uniform and dressed in the one blouse and skirt outfit I had brought from home. My only shoes now were my boots, but I had to have something on my feet. Without my uniform and beret, I felt strangely bare. But Esteban had forbidden us to wear boots outside the house. I sighed and gathered the clothes that needed washing, put them in the basket, and started out the door. Veronica stopped scrubbing Isabel's face and looked at me. "Where are you going?"

"The washing . . ."

"Not today," she said. "We can do it another time."

"It's all right. We can't let them stop us." I think I even tossed my head. "I'm not afraid." Which of course was a colossal lie.

"Well, *I'm* afraid," she said quietly. She took the basket from my hands. "Please . . ."

Perhaps I should have argued, but I didn't. I wasn't that bold.

"Rafael is eager to write his name," she said. "He wants to be like his papi. Would you teach him?"

"Of course," I said. "When?"

"Now is a good time."

I went out and found Rafael squatting between two rows of tobacco plants, pulling bugs off the leaves and dropping them into a cup of kerosene. Luis, usually busy in the fields, was nowhere to be seen. I remember thinking that he must have gone to the Acostas' for something.

Rafael was delighted to leave his messy chore to have a private lesson with the grown-ups' teacher. We went back into the house.

"Sit at the table," I said. "Your mama said you wanted to write your name. You have a long name with many letters. Can you do that?"

He nodded vigorously.

I fetched my diary and two pencils from my rucksack. Then I sat on a stool next to him, tore a page from the back of my diary, and carefully wrote his name on it.

"See?" I said. "You have a very hard name to write."

He studied the paper and then carefully took up a pencil. He worked with his eyes squeezed in concentration. His mouth was open and his tongue went back and forth across his lips as though willing his fingers to push the pencil across the page.

His first attempts looped and straggled like drunken snakes. One attempt even left the page entirely and ended up marking the tabletop.

"Maybe we should wait until you've learned your letters."

"No." He shook his head. "No. I can do it." I tore a fresh piece of paper from the back of the diary, and he began again.

Within the hour, he could copy his name well enough that I could read each letter. We called Veronica in. "Oh!" she said with that expression I'd often seen on my mother's face when confronted with her child's small triumph. "I see the maestra has written your name."

"No!" Rafael cried. "It was me! Can you believe that? I did it myself."

"But this is wonderful!" she said and kissed his beaming cheek. "You are such a clever boy!"

"He's very clever," I said. "And he worked very hard. I think he has earned his own notebook and pencil." I got a spare notebook from my gear and handed it to him along with one of the pencils.

"For me?"

"Yes. But now you must come to class every night. Those are not toys for you to play with. You have to be a real student."

He looked at his mother. "Truly? Every night with you and Papi and the Acostas?"

"Of course," she said. "If you have a notebook and pencil, you have to be a serious learner."

Afterward, I went out and helped him in the tobacco patch. The work had to be done.

"Where did Luis go?" I asked Veronica when we came into the house.

"He had some business in the town," she said.

It was nearly dark when he returned. He had bought a heavy metal bolt. Without a word he fastened it to the inside of the front door.

That night, with the help of Daniel and the others, we rearranged the house. The two mattresses now lay across the kitchen floor, and the kitchen table, with stools around it, stood in what had been the bedroom. The lantern hung over the table, and my hammock and blanket were neatly folded in a corner with my rucksack on top.

Before we began the nightly lesson, Veronica asked for the loan of my blanket, which she hung over the tiny back window before she lit the lantern. Then she draped another blanket over the light curtain that hung from the doorway between the two rooms.

"Bandidos?" Dunia asked.

"No word of them," said Luis. "But it's better to be careful, yes?"

It was a hot night and stultifying in that airless room. Everyone was sweating, but again, no one complained.

A week came and went. We continued to work in the back room, but with each passing day, the fears eased. Rafael was a happy addition to the class. He learned so quickly, and no one wanted to be left behind by a six-year-old. Luis and Nancy took the first exam and both got a perfect score. I planned to go to the Sunday meeting and share this good news, but a farmer from that area stopped by with the message that there was to be no meeting that week.

The following Sunday, however, we met as usual. The runaways had been spotted far away from our area, so the militia felt that the immediate danger had passed. I was able to go to our meeting and tell about Dunia's triumph, as well as get some hints about how to help the others move forward through their first exams. I was proud of my little class. I told them how Rafael was inspiring everyone with his excitement and the way he caught on quickly to everything.

To add to my delight, there was a letter from my father. He said they had been glad to get four letters from me on one day. Everyone was well, they missed me, and was I all right? Because, if not, there was no shame if I wanted to come home.

On the back of Papi's letter, my little brother, Roberto, had written his own, which I was able to make out despite the smudges and strange spelling.

Dear Lora,

I am fine. How are you? I am proud to tell everyone that my sister is a Conrado Benítez Brigadista. I am also happy to say we are going to have a long vacation from school so our teachers can join the campaign. Silvio wants to join, but Mama cried, so he gave it up. I want to join, too, but Papi says they do not want seven-year-olds who cannot write a single sentence without misspelling three words. Come home soon. I miss you.

Love,

Your brother, Roberto Díaz Llera

Several others had gotten letters, too. We all read our letters out loud, so that those who received no mail could pretend that they had had news from home as well. When I read Roberto's news that his school was to be closed, Esteban interrupted me.

"Yes, I was to share that news with you. The government has temporarily closed schools and the teachers will join us. Midyear reports discovered that the campaign is behind schedule, so we need more trained teachers in the field if we are to meet our goal."

There was no need for me to worry about my brothers missing a bit of school. Papi would take care of that. He was so determined that his children have more learning than he had. Over the years, he had bought books whenever he had a few extra pesos. He wouldn't allow those boys to get behind in their studies. He'd have them reading everything in our little home library and quizzing them on it. He'd make them long for ordinary school days. And if there were many more teachers as slow as I was, the campaign needed teachers more than my little brothers did.

Maria had received a letter, but she didn't share it. If I had paid closer attention to my friend, I would have realized that something was wrong, but I was too involved in my own thoughts of family and the pleasure of being with the squad again.

It felt like a good meeting to me. Most of us

thought that our students were doing well, but the goal-driven Esteban reminded us that it was already August. Four more months and the year would be over. If we did not reach our goal, "We shall prevail" would turn into "We gave it a try."

I was sure he was talking to me. He knew quite well that only two of my now seven students had passed their second exams. Veronica, Daniel, and Rafael were nearly there, but none of the Acostas had even passed their first. I was determined that Daniel pass his second exam immediately. If I hinted that Rafael was nearly ready to take his exam, Daniel was bound to try harder.

Astride Bonita's back, with Maria sitting behind me on the broad saddle, I thought I heard a sniff. "Are you all right, Maria?"

Her answer was blurred by her sobs. "My parents . . ." she began.

"Did you get bad news from home?"

"Yes," she said.

All I could think of was someone dying. How awful it would be if Abuela or one of my parents

would die when I was so far away. "Did someone die?"

"Worse."

It was hard for me to imagine anything worse.
"What is it?" I tried to turn backward in the saddle
enough to see her face, but she had covered it with
her hands.

"They forbid me." She began to cry in earnest. "I
should never have sent that picture to them."

I waited for more.

"They are angry with me. They say Enrico must
be Haitian, he is so black."

"Oh." It was all I could think to say.

"I can't give him up! I love him with all my
heart!" She was blubbering now.

I wanted to ask how she could give him up when
there was no evidence that he had ever been hers.
That might have been true, but it seemed terribly
unkind.

"I'm sorry." It was all I could think to say.

* * *

On Monday night, I sounded like Esteban, reminding my students that our motto was "We shall prevail." "And that means," I said, "everyone! *Everyone* has to finish the primer before I leave in December or I will be counted a failure as your teacher."

"No, no," Dunia protested. "No one tries as hard as you. You are a wonderful teacher. It is not your fault if you do not have clever students."

"You are a very clever student, Dunia. I know you can finish the primer. And Joaquin, you *have* to finish, so you can write your complaint to Fidel."

Daniel passed his second exam on Tuesday night and Rafael and Veronica the following night. By Saturday, the elderly Acostas had passed their first exams, not with perfect scores, but decent ones. Greatly relieved, I gave my report to Esteban and Lilian. "Good work, but you need to work harder," Esteban said. "It's practically September."

On the way home that afternoon, Maria said, "I told Enrico that my parents didn't approve of our relationship. I didn't want to, but I thought he should know. I always think it is best to be honest, don't you?"

"Really? You told him? And what did he say?" I was trying hard to imagine how surprised poor Enrico might have been to find out a love affair was over before he knew it had begun.

"He said"—she interjected a sob between the words—"he said he thought it would be wise for us to just be friends."

"Oh," I said.

"Just friends!" she said, and burst into fresh tears.

I had what I thought at the moment was a brilliant idea. "You should write a poem about it," I said.

"A poem?"

"Yes, a poem. When your heart is broken, poetry can be very healing."

"Do you really think so?"

"You should try," I said, and promptly forgot about it, as life soon began to speed up for all of us.

* * *

The first thing that happened was not the most important, but it did mark a milestone in my life. It began the first week of September with an ache in my stomach and a slight backache. When I visited the outdoor toilet, I realized what was happening. Girls at school often talked about it. But I didn't know what to do. I was totally unprepared. There were no pharmacies in the mountains. I was embarrassed, but the only thing I could do was ask Veronica for help. She was so kind, just like the older sister I'd described for my parents. She got me the makeshift rags that women in the country must use in such times. "Now you are a woman, Lora," she said, "not just a teacher."

I couldn't remember that she'd ever called me by my name before.

CHAPTER THIRTEEN

The Accident

AT THE SANTANAS' FARM, SEPTEMBER 1961

Far more important than that milestone in my life was what happened soon afterward. It didn't matter how often Luis or Veronica protested, I couldn't shake the feeling that the accident was my fault. I had written a letter home telling my family about my students' progress, and I was anxious to get it sent. I fussed aloud at breakfast that the letters I gave to Esteban and Lilian for mailing took forever to arrive in Havana.

"Veronica," Luis said as he was getting up from the table, "I noticed we have more guava fruit than we can eat. We haven't used all our rations. I think I'll go to market and sell some of the guava. Then I could buy more rice. If you like, Lora, I could mail your letter for you while I'm there."

He borrowed the Acostas' old mare to take a large burlap sack of guava fruit and my letter. He got safely to town, bought the rice, and secured the bag to Bonita's saddle. It was on the way home that the accident occurred.

Bonita, as I've said before, was the slowest, kindest horse in the Western Hemisphere. But sweet old Bonita had thrown Luis into the brush.

"It was not her fault," Luis said to us afterward. "She was startled. You would jump, too, if a large boa suddenly appeared at your feet." When Luis had tried to stand, he told us, his right leg had buckled under his body and the pain in his back and leg had forced him to lie down again at once.

"But I couldn't just lie there and wait for a snake

to bite or mosquitoes to eat me," he said. "So I called Bonita and somehow got myself onto the saddle. She was very sorry. I could tell how sorry she was. She stood very still and gazed sadly at me while I struggled up on her back, and she was very careful and gentle all the rest of the way home."

Veronica and I helped him to their mattress. He winced when we got him down on his back. Veronica and I knelt on either side of the patient. She carefully took off his shirt and pushed up his pants' leg. His leg was bloody. The children were standing around the mattress. Rafael was trying bravely not to cry—to be like his papi, but when the girls saw the blood, they both burst into tears.

"Shh," Luis said. "Don't cry. Papi will be fine."

I knew there was nothing I could do about his back except pray it wasn't broken, but when Veronica washed the blood off his leg, it was so strangely twisted that I felt sure it was broken. Luis was trying so hard to smile, to make a brave front for the sake of the children, but it was apparent that he was in agony. I made him swallow a couple of aspirin—the best I could do for the pain. "We need to get you to a doctor," I said.

"I can't go to a doctor," he said. "I'll be all right. Just let me rest a bit."

"I'll fetch Esteban," Rafael said.

Everyone looked at him. "It's nearly dark," Veronica said. "And it's a long way."

"I know the way," the boy said. "I'll ride Bonita."

"No," I said. "I'll go."

Luis reached out his hand and grasped my arm. "If someone must go, it would be better if it's the boy. The bandidos aren't looking for him."

Not long after Rafael set out, the Acostas came for the lessons. "Is everything all right?" Daniel asked as soon as Veronica unbolted the door. "I didn't see the horse."

"Mother of God!" In the dim light of the kitchen, Dunia had made out the form of Luis lying on one of the mattresses. "What is this?"

"There was a little accident," Luis said, trying to get into a sitting position. "Don't worry. The horse wasn't hurt. Rafael insisted on taking her to fetch Esteban." He clinched his teeth and lowered himself slowly back down. "Though what can *he* do more than cluck his teeth? A little rest, and I'll be fine. Now, go to the back room and do your lessons. I can listen from here."

When Esteban arrived, he tried to persuade Luis that he should see a doctor, but it would mean a journey of more than a day, and Luis was adamant. So Esteban improvised a splint for Luis's leg and told him sternly not to try to stand on it until Esteban could somehow fetch a doctor to come examine him and encase his leg in a proper cast.

"But who will plow tomorrow?" he asked.

"I will," said Rafael.

I took the child's hand. "We will," I said. "We'll make a good team. You'll see."

And the next day, we did. The boy's arms could not reach across to both handles of the plow, so he led the oxen while I guided the plow. I tried not to think of Luis, lying in pain on the kitchen floor. I kept trying to tell myself that it was an accident. That it was not my fault that Luis had decided to go to the market. That no one could have predicted that a snake would spook the horse and he would be thrown. But somehow the sweat pouring down my face was not only for the physical exertion of pushing the plow.

When we looked at our efforts at the end of the morning, it was plain to see that our furrows were far from straight, but it was the best we could do.

Veronica had made rice and beans for us. Even though she had my ration card as well as the family's, I always tried to eat sparingly of food we had not grown ourselves — like that rice that nearly cost Luis his life. But I didn't have to hold back that day. I had no appetite.

"Don't peck at your food like a chicken," Veronica said. "You need to eat more. You are working hard."

"See?" Rafael said. "I'm not eating like a chicken. I'm eating like Gordo." Gordo was the fattest of the four pigs.

His mother laughed. "You're always eating like Gordo."

Veronica and I carefully propped Luis up to a sitting position so he could eat his food. My whole body flinched watching the pain in his face, but he emptied his plate, gave a crooked smile, and slid back to the mattress. "Like a baby," he said. "So helpless."

Is it too hard? Yes, I thought, but it's not the work. It is too hard to see this suffering and know I had a part in it. But I can't run from it. I am needed now for more than teaching the ABCs.

When it was time for lessons that night, Luis asked Rafael to fetch his pencil and workbook. "At least I can study while I'm lying here useless," he said to me.

"Not useless," I said, suddenly realizing that with concentrated work, he could finish the primer quickly. "And as soon as you have written your letter to Fidel," I said, "you can help me by teaching the others."

"Me? A teacher?"

"Oh, yes, Luis. You will be a fine teacher."

* * *

When the following week Esteban came, escorting the doctor, I was able to give him Luis's final exam, including his letter to Fidel Castro. The signature, *Luis Santana,* was large and bold.

The doctor said Luis's back was badly bruised but not fractured. He put a proper cast on Luis's leg and provided him with crutches so he could hobble around a bit, though he warned Luis against trying to walk any distance, and working in the fields was forbidden.

Esteban echoed the doctor's instructions. "I know that will be hard for you, Luis," he said. "You have worked hard all your life."

"Oh," said Luis. "I haven't stopped working."

"But . . ." both Esteban and the doctor began to sputter in protest.

"Yes," said Luis. "I'm working hard. I have a new job. I have become a teacher. It keeps me very busy."

CHAPTER FOURTEEN

Too Hard

OCTOBER 1961

It was still the rainy season, with showers every day, but we did not stop work or lessons because of rain. In Havana, we might have stayed indoors until the shower passed. In the mountains we just kept on working, rain or shine. Of course we tried to bring the laundry in so it wouldn't get soaked again, but with all that was going on, we didn't always succeed.

In the country, no one worries about the rainy season. But hurricanes are another matter. And it turned out that 1961 was a bumper year for hurricanes. They began in July and didn't end until November. Every time we got word that Hurricane Anna or Betsy or Carla or one of their sisters was on the way, I began to be anxious — not only for what a storm like that would do to the crops but also for what would happen to the house itself. Tropical hurricanes had blown away stronger houses than ours. Luckily, even though several hurricanes hit Cuba on the west or the east, causing flooding and death, we in the central mountains were largely undamaged by the rains and winds. Our threats did not come from nature.

We had never given up being careful — Luis wouldn't let us — but when weeks had gone by without a hint of trouble, I decided that I should certainly now be able to go to the river for water or washing. After all, just the day before, Maria and I had gone to our Sunday meeting. We were all back to wearing our uniforms. Our singing and dancing was joyful. No one had to pull me to my feet to join in. What's more, Esteban had praised Luis's final exam and read aloud his letter to Castro before the whole squad. My friends all clapped, and someone shouted, "Hooray, Lora!" I tried not to blush. It was Luis's triumph, not mine.

On the way home, I was feeling particularly happy. When we got to Maria's house, she asked me to wait. She wanted to show me her poem.

I was so eager to get home that I didn't even dismount. She ran into the house and came back with a page obviously torn from her diary. "Here," she said. "Poetry has not healed me, but then," she sighed, "nothing will. But anyhow . . ." She handed the paper up to me.

"I'll read it on the way home," I said. I didn't want to have to read it with her standing right there waiting for me to comment on it. And it was a good thing I decided to wait. Well, let me just say that Maria was a much better literacy teacher than a poet. I could hardly keep from laughing out loud as I bounced along on Bonita's back—the lines of verse just about as bumpy as the ride.

I could see the pain in his dark eyes.
He sighed and I knew the meaning:
"My heart is broken into a million tiny pieces,"
And the grief in my eyes replied,
"Yes, yes, my heart, too, is broken,
Broken into a million tiny pieces."

On and on it went. I didn't count, but there must have been at least fifty lines echoing this beginning. I mean, just how many times in one poem can you say "My heart is broken into a million tiny pieces"?

There had been no warning of danger, and if not for the animals, we would never have known. We were in the back room as usual that Monday night. My thoughts by then were not on Maria's lost love life, whether real or imagined, or even her lack of poetic talent, but on my students.

Nancy was busy writing and rewriting her letter. She had pushed herself to finish her exams because next month her baby would be born. Writing the letter was proving much harder for her than the rest of the exam. She was something of a perfectionist and could not tolerate a single erasure. "Look," she said disgustedly, "you can still see the mistake underneath. I need to do it over. It has to be beautiful if it is to go to Havana."

Rafael was racing Daniel and his mother, determined to beat them both through the primer, and Daniel was just as determined not to let a six-year-old triumph. I was beginning to have real hope that most, if not all, of my students would complete their three exams before December.

I was working hard with Dunia, and Luis, as usual, was tutoring Joaquin. The elder Acostas had finally passed their second exams but were struggling with the lessons leading to the third.

"Nothing but long words!" Joaquin complained loudly. "I can read the little ones, but now they are all as long as a water snake!"

I could hardly disagree. He had gone from words like *house* and *hill* to words like *industry* and *revolutionary government*. A bit of a distance for an old man who had first met the alphabet just a few months earlier.

Luis broke the words into syllables and drilled the old man until he was nearly crying for mercy. But Luis was a stern teacher who wasted no pity. "If you don't learn these words, you can't write your letter to Fidel, and poor Lora will go home feeling like a failure. Besides," he added, "do you want your wife to finish first? Dunia is not letting the long words defeat her. Remember! Our motto is 'We shall prevail,' not 'We tried but the words were too long, so we whined and gave up.'"

"But even if I learn the words, you say I have to make these little marks over some, but not all of the letters, and to put a squiggle above the *en-ye*!" the old man complained. "That's too much for my old brains to remember. I guess those evil Spaniards invented all that as well?"

"Yes," said Luis, "I'm sure they did, but now they make good Cuban words. Besides, I think the marks and squiggle, as you say, are pretty. Would you want your language to look as dull and undecorated as North American English?"

I was almost beginning to think it was a good thing that Luis had broken his leg. He was such a help, and I knew I needed a lot if I was going to get all of them through the last test before the end of the campaign.

We were deep into our lessons. Veronica was determined to pass her final exam before her son did, and I was in the middle of the dictation section when Luis suddenly said, "Hush!" I stopped reading aloud, and we all listened. "The animals," he whispered. "Something is out there." And then we all heard them. The chickens were cackling excitedly, the pigs were squealing, and even the oxen and goats were making anxious bleats. Luis grabbed a crutch and, as he struggled to his feet, whispered, "Douse the lamp, somebody." Daniel jumped up to obey. Luis pushed back from the table, shoved aside the blanket, and stumped his way into the kitchen.

The animal protests grew louder. Then we

heard shouting and a *bam, bam, bam* on the front door.

"Open up! We know you have a brigadista in there!"

For a moment we sat there, frozen. Then Rafael let out a muffled cry: "Mama." Veronica put her arm around him.

"Shh."

The banging and yelling continued. Suddenly it was interrupted by Luis's voice.

"I will not open my door to criminals. But be aware that I also have a rifle, and if you bandidos try to enter this house, you will not see another morning!" I never knew Luis to own a rifle, but he was banging on the back of the door with something that sounded like the point of a gun.

There was some muffled talking outside. And again Luis's strong voice: "If you try to break in, just remember, I'm in the dark and you're in the moonlight. You won't see who's killed you until you reach the gates of hell!"

There were a few more half-hearted *bams* on the

door and then "We'll be back!" There were more threats thrown back at the house as, apparently, the insurgents drifted toward the woods. I thought I heard in the distance the sound of a piglet squealing.

When only the chirp of insects broke the silence of the night, Luis came back into the bedroom. Daniel relit the lamp and revealed Luis standing in the doorway with a broom in his hand. He dropped it and gave an embarrassed titter. "I guess I can let go of my weapon now," he said sheepishly.

For a long while, we sat silently around the table. Finally Daniel stood up. "It's safe to go," he announced. "And we have animals to care for in the morning." We all went out to watch them go, peering anxiously toward the dark forest. When they disappeared into the shadows, we stepped back in and Luis bolted the door. On her mattress, Isabel turned over with a sigh. I looked down. The little girls had slept through it all.

"Sleep if you can, Lora," Luis said. "The animals will wake me if there's danger."

It was a hot October night and the air in the

small back room was stuffy. But I lay shivering in my hammock, as cold as a fish on ice. From the woods, an owl screeched. I jumped. *I won't be fourteen until November 5th. I am too young to die.* I don't think I said the words aloud, but they were pounding as noisily in my head as if I had. I pulled my almost-forgotten rosary out from under my nightdress and tried to smother my fear with a succession of whispered Our Fathers and Hail Marys. *Dear Mother of God, don't let me die out here so far from my own mother. Even, even if they don't kill me, won't I be putting my beloved new family in danger just by being here?*

It's too hard! The thought hit me like a bullet to the chest. I had promised to go home when it got too hard.

CHAPTER FIFTEEN

The Decision

LATE OCTOBER 1961

By morning, I had made up my mind. Luis's leg was nearly healed. He could take over my teaching job. I had done the work I'd come to do. There would be no shame in leaving a few weeks earlier than scheduled. Next Sunday, when I went to the meeting, I would tell Lilian about the threat. I had the feeling she would be more sympathetic than Esteban. I'd ask her to send word to my father. In the meantime, I wouldn't say anything to the family. I would work harder than ever, and then when my father came to fetch me, I would tell the Santanas that I must go home.

I told myself that it was not only my own safety that I was fearful for. As long as I was in their home, they were all in danger. This time the insurgents had made off with a small pig and a few chickens, but when they came back—who knew what they would do? A broom banging against the door might not fool them a second time.

Veronica was the only one who expressed grief for the lost chickens, but the little girls cried over the piglet. They had named him Oscar, and Emilia was sure he hated being kidnapped by those "bad men." Rafael was happy that at least Gordo, his favorite pig, was much too fat to be carried away.

By Wednesday, someone—Daniel? Joaquin? Veronica? Surely not Luis, still on crutches until the doctor came in November—had gotten word to Esteban about the incident. Word came back that all brigadistas were to stay in their houses until further notice—not to go outside, not even to go into the close-by fields to work.

I caught up on my diary notes. I started to reread *Pride and Prejudice*. I was glad all over again that I had brought the original English. It would take much longer to reread than if it were in Spanish. Veronica and Rafael were doing the outdoor work, so I did as much of the housework as she would let me and taught the eager Emilia the entire alphabet in one day. Luis was tutoring Rafael when his son could be spared from the field, so I couldn't be of much help there.

There was, of course, no meeting on Sunday, but to my surprise, Esteban appeared at our door that afternoon. He asked me to come outdoors and speak to him privately. It was a relief to get out and smell the fresh air and see the sun shining on the fields and woods. Veronica and Rafael were bent over the bean patch. I longed to join them.

"Lora . . . Lora?" I turned my attention to Esteban.

"I'm sorry. It just feels so good to be out of the house. It's such a beautiful time of year."

"Yes," he said. "But maybe not for you." I must have looked startled.

"I know you've had a very frightening experience. Lilian reminded me that you're still only thirteen. No one will blame you if you go home a little early."

"Go home?" I hadn't asked to go home—yet. "Go home?" I repeated myself, trying to untangle this unexpected twist. It was supposed to be my decision, not Esteban's.

At that moment, Emilia came running out of the house and grabbed the leg of my uniform. "Lora! Lora!" she cried. "Isabel can do the ABCs all the way to *g*! I taught her myself! I'm a teacher just like you!"

Little Isabel came out, her hand in front of her face. "Say your alphabet for Lora, Isabel!" her sister commanded.

Isabel said something behind her hand. Emilia snatched it away from her face. "Lora can't hear you! Say it again!"

I knelt down beside her and put my arm around her. She smiled a tiny smile and whispered into my ear, "A-b-c-ch-d-e-f-g—that's all I know."

"That's wonderful," I whispered back, and kissed her cheek. I was conscious of Esteban watching us, so I stood up. "Will it be too dangerous for them if I stay?"

He shook his head. "We can't be sure, but I don't think so," he said. "The militia will keep a close eye if I ask."

I stroked Isabel's hair and smiled at proud Emilia. "I can't leave them," I said. "I promised."

Chapter Sixteen

Celebrations

NOVEMBER 1961

It proved to be Oscar that led to the capture of the insurgents who had threatened our home. They made the mistake of butchering the piglet, and the smell of roasting pork and the sight of smoke alerted the militia to the bandits' location. Juan and the other young boys were gleeful when they talked about it. "They didn't even get a bite of meat before they became a feast for the vultures." Juan was chortling as he said this. I put my hand in front of my mouth, afraid I might throw up.

I never had the heart to tell Emilia and Isabel what had happened to their beloved Oscar. Of course, the children were farm raised. They knew perfectly well where their occasional dishes with meat came from. Even I had seen chickens slaughtered. And before I left, a piglet and a small goat would join celebrations, and not as guests. It was the idea that the bandidos had made off with *Oscar* that distressed the little girls. I could not tell them about his ironic end. They would not have cheered.

Poor Maria! She was still lamenting her mistake of sending the picture of herself and Enrico to her parents. "Now he hardly speaks to me. 'Just friends'! What does it mean to be just friends?"

She nearly drowned poor old Bonita with her tears. "Writing a poem didn't help at all," she said. Fortunately she didn't ask me for my opinion of her poetry. It might have set me off, and no one with a broken heart wants a friend laughing in her face. She was so unhappy those days.

As for me, the next few weeks proved to be my

happiest time in the mountains. First, there was my fourteenth birthday, on November 5. Somehow the family knew the date, and that night after our lessons, they told me to close my eyes and wait. After much giggling, Emilia and Isabel came to the back room. Each of them took one of my hands, and they led me carefully around the mattresses in the front room and out the door. "Now you can open your eyes," Emilia said.

I opened my eyes to a large bonfire blazing in the yard in front of the house. There were a lot of people standing there. A few people tried a ragged English version of "Happy Birthday to You" (somehow it's a song people think can only be sung in English), but soon they abandoned the attempt and burst into a song our music teacher in school had told us was beloved by the people in these mountains. Its refrain, "Son de la loma," means "They come from the hills."

Juan, and then Maria, were there with their own students. I could see in the firelight that even in the midst of her own sadness, Maria was smiling for me.

Esteban and Lilian were there, too. The folks from the neighboring farms had brought food and drink. We danced and sang until late into the night. The campesinos taught us mountain dances that we city kids had never seen before, and Maria urged Juan and me to show our friends dances that we did in the city. Well, to be honest, I was stumbling all over my feet trying to follow Maria's lead. Among all her other assets, her ability to dance absolutely shone. Everyone was laughing and clapping with delight.

I didn't care how poorly I danced. I had never felt so honored or so happy. Lying in my hammock, feeling too full of food and music to sleep, I thought how close I had come to missing this night of nights.

Two days later, Bonita came galloping, or as close to galloping as the old mare could manage, with Daniel on her back. "The baby is coming! The baby is coming!" he cried, which meant that they had sent him to fetch Veronica to help Dunia with the birth.

"May I come?" I asked Veronica shyly.

She looked at me. "You won't be afraid?"

"No, I promise. And I won't get in the way. I just want to be there."

"Then come along," she said. Daniel gave us the horse. He wouldn't be needed, so he would walk. I climbed up on Bonita's back behind Veronica, and off we went, faster than I'd ever ridden before.

"Watch the branches!" Veronica warned.

I, of course, had been watching the path for snakes, but I heard her warning just in time to duck.

Being there when Nancy's baby was born—oh, how can I explain it? It was being allowed to witness a miracle. He was a squalling, little wriggly boy. They let me hold him while they tended to Nancy after his birth. That was when I decided. I would go back to the city and get the education I needed to become a doctor. My country needed more doctors, and I wanted not only to help heal; I wanted to help bring new life into the world.

On the 15th, the real doctor came and took off Luis's cast. His leg was ashen and shriveled, but the doctor was confident that the bone had healed well, and he was sure that with exercise, the muscles would grow strong and Luis would be "as good as new" or "maybe even better with a doctor like me," he said with a laugh. (I told myself that when *I* became a doctor, I would not brag, not even as a joke.) My now mature fourteen-year-old self was sure that doctors and priests as well as teachers should always be sincere and humble.

CHAPTER SEVENTEEN

¡Venceremos!

NOVEMBER–DECEMBER 1961

We were still gathered at the base camp on Sunday, November 26. Our work was done, and Carlos was leading the singing. Maria and Isora were, as usual, getting us all into the dancing. By this date, many of the campesinos were joining us as soon as they heard the music.

We didn't hear the hoofbeats, but suddenly there was the horseman riding into the village. He leaped off the horse, raced over to Esteban, and pulled him out of the circle. The music stopped as suddenly as if someone had pulled the plug from a radio. The man was in a militia uniform and was whispering, but his gestures were huge and wild. To a person, we all stood there, just staring. *What was wrong? Something terrible must have happened.* My heart felt like a stone banging in my chest. Little Isora grabbed my hand. I squeezed hers. Not to reassure but to share the fear.

At length, Esteban nodded and turned back toward us. He cleared his throat. "It's bad news," he said. "One of our brigadistas has been murdered."

Someone—Maria, I think—let out a cry. I was too frozen to make a sound.

"His name," Esteban continued, "is . . . was . . . Manuel Ascunce." He looked around, wanting to see if the name meant something to any of the squad. No one spoke, so he went on. "He was working and teaching on the Palmarito coffee farm. His campesino host was also killed." He waited to let us take in this cruel fact before he continued. "The funeral for Manuel will be tomorrow in the capital."

Isora let go of my hand and began to sob, as did

many of the others. Even the boys were seen to hide their faces so their tears would not show. Maria was weeping openly, but my sobs choked in my throat. I knew how terrified I would have been had the bandits gotten past our door.

"We are—" Esteban began, but had to stop to clear his throat again. "We are all devastated by this news. And perhaps frightened." As he said this, he seemed to be looking at me and little Isora trembling at my side. "But I believe we must carry on."

"¡Venceremos!" I think it was Carlos who called out our familiar slogan. *We shall prevail!* And then we all echoed the shout. Even I was somehow able to get the syllables past my parched throat. "¡Venceremos!"

"Yes, indeed," said Esteban. "Yes, truly. ¡Venceremos!"

The details of the killing became clearer on subsequent Sundays. Manuel Ascunce was sixteen years old. He was barely two years my senior, but in courage much, much older. A band of insurgents appeared at the farm where he was teaching, and

Manuel, hoping to save his students, stepped forward. "I am the teacher," he said. But they took both him and Pedro Lantiqua, his host father, whom they knew to be a strong supporter of Fidel, away to the forest, where they tortured them, killed them, and hung their bodies from an acacia tree.

Manuel has become a celebrated martyr, the brigadista who gave his life to the cause. Later, schools and hospitals would bear his name. But I'm sorry to say I knew that day in my heart that I would rather be a live coward than a dead hero.

There was a great parade, a somber celebration, in Havana. Brigadistas and ordinary citizens crowded the streets of the capital as the body of Manuel Ascunce was carried to his grave. Those of us so far away could not be there, but all that day he was in our minds.

At the time, I thought I remembered seeing him in Varadero. We were probably there at the same time for training, weren't we? Maybe I had seen him among the many thousands there. Both Maria and Juan swore we'd been at the same camp. Juan even said he'd spoken to him once. I found out much later that Manuel had been at the training camp at an entirely different time. By now I have seen so many pictures of him that it's hard to believe I never saw him in the flesh. Who knows? Maybe I saw him once in Havana before we both joined the campaign. His home was not so far from my old neighborhood. I'd like to think I saw him once. Is that peculiar? Don't we all want to feel we have touched greatness?

After Manuel Ascunce's death, none of us would admit to wanting to go home. He had given his life for the campaign. We had to finish the year in his honor. By early December, everyone in my group except Joaquin and Dunia had finished his or her final exams, including the required letter to Castro. I missed having Nancy and Daniel in class, but they were at home taking care of little José. They named him after our national hero from the war of independence from Spain. But José Martí, as I tried to explain earlier, is not just our George Washington, who fought for independence, or our Abraham Lincoln, who fought for freedom and against slavery.

Martí was also, as you know, a great poet and a philosopher.

When Luis passed his final exam, I gave him my book of José Martí's poems. They were precious to me, but I knew that when I got back to Havana, I could buy another copy. I often wondered if Manuel Ascunce thought of "The White Rose" when he was dying. Here is my English translation of the poem I love so much:

> I grow a white rose,
> In July as well as January,
> To give to my true friend
> Who offers me his honest hand.
>
> And for the one whose cruel blows
> Break the heart that gives me life,
> I cultivate neither thistle nor thorn:
> I grow a white rose.

I could not think of the poem without at the same time thinking of Norma. Did she still love

José Martí? Or was she now enamored with North American poets? Was it easier for her to be a black American than it had been to be a black Cuban? Would I ever see her again in this lifetime? My grief for Manuel Ascunce was mixed up with my mourning for my lost friend.

Luis knew how distressed all the brigadistas in the area were, so he made a special trip to the nearest church where there was still a priest and begged him to come soon so that little José could be baptized and we could have a joyful celebration as an antidote to our sadness.

Dunia, with Veronica's help, prepared a great feast with as much food as they had made for my birthday. The other host families in the area were invited to celebrate with us at the Acostas' farm, so they brought food as well. Our whole squad was there, and there was some comfort for us that night in little José's presence. You cannot look at a tiny baby and feel entirely hopeless. We passed him from one uniformed set of arms to another. Even the most macho of the boys wanted a turn.

I saw that night why poor Maria was so in love with Enrico. I had never seen a boy look at a baby with such a tender, loving gaze. I was so happy to see Maria smiling when her turn came to hold baby José. I think it was the first time many of us had smiled since we'd heard the news of Manuel's death.

"But if you really want to see Lora smile her beautiful smile," Luis said to Joaquin and Dunia, "you have to pass your final exams, and write your letter to Fidel before she leaves."

We were slated to leave on December 20. It was now the second week of December. Dunia was almost ready, but she would insist on repeating a lesson even when I felt sure she was ready to move on. She sensed that I was losing patience with her. I didn't mean to, but I so needed her to pass, and I was sure she could if she tried hard enough. One night when Joaquin and Luis were noisily at work, she whispered in my ear. "I must wait. Old men, they feel the loss of their machismo, don't you see?" I could only sigh and nod.

So I cheered heartily when on December 15, Luis declared that Joaquin was at last ready to take his final exam. The old man passed, not brilliantly like his daughter-in-law or almost perfectly like his son, but he passed and was set to work writing the long-awaited letter to our country's leader.

December 15, 1961
Dr. Fidel Castro
City of Havana
Comrade Fidel:

I can read and write, even the big words and the squiggle on *en-ye.* But why must I write my name like the old Spanish oppressors? We won independence. We won the revolution. We have won the war against illiteracy. Now we must free our spelling.

Your comrade,
Joaquin Acosta

"That's a wonderful letter, Joaquin," I said.

"I'll write a better one next year, when I know more big words," he said. "That will surprise him, won't it?"

"I'm sure it will," I said, eager to get back to my final student.

Dunia waited a discreet three days before she agreed to try her exam. We never told anyone that her grade was higher than her husband's.

CHAPTER EIGHTEEN

¡Vencimos!

LEAVING THE MOUNTAINS, DECEMBER 1961

Too soon, it was the 20th of December. Nancy and Daniel did not go to see me off because of little José as well as farm duties, and Veronica stayed home because she said it would be a long day and someone had to look after the animals. She hugged me tight and kissed me, then turned away so I wouldn't see her tears. "Lorita, you must thank your kind papi and mama for lending us their wonderful daughter for this year," she said. Which made me burst into tears. She was so beautiful, my sister Veronica, as lovely as any statue of the Madonna in the cathedral.

She waved good-bye as the rest of the family and I went on to the Acostas', so that I could say good-bye to Daniel and Nancy and the baby I almost thought of as my own.

"Bonita insists on coming, too," said Joaquin as he and Dunia mounted the big saddle on the mare's back. We already made quite a little parade to the base camp, where we met our squad and most of their host families. There the parade swelled into a small army making its way through the trees and vegetation that crowded both sides of the path.

Rafael ran and skipped ahead with some of the other boys, but often threaded the crowd to come back to check on me and his family. Soon Isabel begged for a ride on her father's shoulders, but Emilia, with an air of importance, took my hand as though I needed her to guide my way. Together we made the trek through the forest to the place at the end of the track where the departure truck was already waiting for us.

When she spotted the truck, Isabel climbed down from her father's shoulders and ran to me, clinging to my right leg. Emilia tightened her tiny grip on the hand she had held for the whole journey, as though holding me tight would keep me from leaving.

When the driver said we must go, I was crying again. Both girls saw my tears and began to wail. I knelt down beside them. "This is not good-bye forever," I said. "I'll come back to see you — I promise."

They wiped their hands across their wet faces and tried to smile. "Soon?"

"As soon as I can," I said. "But I have to go back to see my other family in Havana. I have been gone a long time. I don't want them to forget me."

Emilia giggled.

But Isabel was distressed. "Will they forget?"

"Well, maybe my naughty brothers will."

"If those bad boys forget you, you come right back here!"

"Okay," I said. "But I still have to go to school. And Fidel Castro has promised that soon there will be a school here for you to go to. Then you can write me letters."

Emilia's eyes went wide. "Would you write me a letter?"

"Of course," I said. "I don't want you to forget me."

"I will never forget you," she said. "Isabel might. She's little."

"No, I won't." Isabel shook her head vigorously.

"I'll write you, too," I said, and kissed her first and then her sister.

Rafael was standing by his father, watching us and pretending to be grown up.

I got up and went to him. "I'm afraid I'm just a crybaby, Rafael. Not brave like you."

He blinked and wiped his sleeve across his face, then quickly straightened up. He stretched out his hand in a very manly fashion and shook mine. "Vaya con Dios, Lora," he said — go with God — and then added in a whisper, "Will you write me a letter, too?"

"Of course," I said. "We're a team."

I made my way through the crowd to where the Acostas and Bonita had found a spot to wait. They dismounted and embraced me and told me I must come back again. Perhaps I might live in *their* house the next time. I hugged them and stroked old Bonita's nose.

"Be sure to keep studying," I said.

"Of course," said Joaquin. "I am going to write many more letters to Fidel. He will be amazed at my progress."

Luis waited until all those good-byes had been said, and then he came and kissed me on both cheeks. "You have given us a new life, Maestra," he said. "I will thank you every time I write my name."

I began to cry in earnest then, but the driver called to all of us who were lingering to get on the truck, that it was leaving. Pronto!

Hands came down to help me up onto the crowded truck bed, but I didn't try to sit down. Even if they could not see me, I wanted to wave to my beloved family until the truck turned the first bend in the track and they would no longer be able to see my hand in the air.

On the long bumpy ride to the train station, we were mostly quiet. We could never have dreamed in April how sad we would be in December.

The truck took us all the way to Cienfuegos, where we climbed up into open train cars for the last leg of our journey home. While most of us had sat silent on the truck, a few of us still in tears, no one even wanting to whisper, the scene on the train was a different story.

The warm December sun was shining down on us as we clacked along, and we soon began to turn our hearts toward home. Girls who had makeup dug it out of their rucksacks and began to put on lipstick and maybe a little eyeliner. I took out my comb and pulled it through my tangled hair. We were laughing at ourselves. Inside we felt so utterly transformed, so changed from the children we had been nine months before, but somehow we wanted to look as good as we could on the outside when we met our families. I knew that my mother would be appalled at my skin, now as brown as a coconut. I feared she would never escape the old-school prejudice that prized fair skin in a woman. I looked at my rough, calloused hands and asked anxiously if anyone had any hand cream, but no one did.

As we got close to Havana, the air became electric with excitement. The word was being passed around that the new slogan—the banner we would carry in the parade on December 22—was Vencimos. We have conquered. We have prevailed.

When the train pulled into Havana, I was only one of the thousands of brigadistas pouring out of the train cars and into the street crowded with families. I wondered if I would ever be able to find the ones I was searching for. But my clever brothers had made a large sign, WELCOME HOME, LORA DÍAZ LLERA, and put it on a long pole. I spotted it before long and wriggled my way through hundreds of uniformed bodies to throw my arms around them. My entire family, including Abuela, who hardly ever left our house, had come to the train station. It didn't seem to matter to anyone what I looked like. I was safely home. My mother didn't even mention the condition or color of my skin for two wccks, and by thcn thc dccp tan had bcgun to fade, anyway.

On the shortlist of the best days of my life was the Vencimos parade, culminating in the gathering in the Plaza of the Revolution. There we gathered, more than one hundred thousand strong, looking up at the memorial to José Martí. A few of us were waving banners picturing an open book and proclaiming ¡Vencimos! The rest of us were carrying pencils, huge pencils, almost as tall as we were. I was delighted that my assignment was to carry one of the pencils. I only wish I could have sent my giant pencil to Rafael as a memento.

We were like an army of sharpened pencils marching into the center of the capital among our flags and banners. Around our necks we wore red scarves, across which were printed the words *Territorio libre de analfabetismo* — Illiteracy-free territory. We were the first country in the Western Hemisphere that could make that boast.

We had done it. We had overcome our own fears as well as the illiteracy of our fellow Cubans. How could any of us ever forget that day?

This is the song we sang as we marched to the Plaza of the Revolution:

> We did it, we did it, we did it!
> We triumphed, we triumphed, we triumphed!
> Cuba told the world we would
> And we accomplished it.

> Forward the people of America,
> Forward with socialism.
> Cuba in only one year
> Conquered illiteracy.

> Fidel, Fidel,
> Tell us what else we should do.
> Fidel, Fidel,
> We'll always do our duty.

We did it, we did it, we did it!
We triumphed, we triumphed, we triumphed!
Cuba told the world we would
And we accomplished it.

My brigadista year was the year that changed my life. This was true not only for me but, I daresay, for all of us who left our safe, loving homes to become brigadistas for literacy. I learned what I could be and do. I was no longer an isolated, spoiled little girl of the city. I was a member of a campesino family who loved me and taught me more than I could ever teach them.

I think it is best summed up in the words of a friend and fellow brigadista who said, "I taught the campesinos how to read and write, and they taught me how to be a person."

Epilogue

As I had dreamed that day of José's birth, I became, in time, a doctor. My husband, who had also been a brigadista, is a professor of Latin American literature, and he has always supported my ambitions and my career. He learned in 1961 not to underestimate us girls. We have three lovely children, all grown now, and are looking forward to grandchildren.

I try to go back every year to see the Santanas. Within two years, the government built a school on Luis's old tobacco patch and the children had their own maestro. Rafael graduated from the Agricultural University in Havana and went home to help his father and other campesinos be more productive farmers. Emilia became an engineer, and little Isabel is a mathematics professor, if you can believe it. Luis and Veronica completed the educational program that the government established to follow up on the campaign of 1961. The only thing they ever want me to bring them from Havana is a new book.

And little José, you ask, what became of him? He taught for a while in Santiago de Cuba, but after the old folks died, and as his parents were aging, he brought his family back to the mountains. He is the local maestro in the school on the Santanas' land, and Rafael Santana is his best friend.

Are you wondering why, after all these years, I wanted to share my diary of what happened to me in 1961? It was not to prove to you that my country is perfect. Not all the promises of the revolution have been fulfilled. We have yet to embody the ideal of liberty that José Martí dreamed of.

My country is not perfect, but, then, is yours? Perhaps, however, someone reading my story will better understand both me and the country I love. No, we are not perfect, but we do have a literate, educated population. We do have doctors.

There are not so many doctors in West Africa, and as I write this, many of those amazing doctors and nurses are dying as they care for victims of the dreaded Ebola virus.

Once again my government has called for volunteers — not to teach this time, but to heal. Even though I have never become a hero, do you understand why I choose to go?

Author's Note

When my friend Mary Leahy heard that I was planning a second trip to Cuba, she told me how envious she was. Her brother, Senator Patrick Leahy, had been there several times, seeking to mend relations between our two countries, but she herself had never been. Mary had a special reason for wanting to go. For many years she had been the director of Central Vermont Adult Basic Education. Early in her experience with CVABE, Mary told me, she had learned of the amazingly successful 1961 literacy campaign that turned Cuba into an illiteracy-free country. Although Mary was in Vermont, and not in revolutionary Cuba, she tried in a number of ways to incorporate ideas from the Cuban model, including enlisting volunteer teachers with the humility to know that they would be learning alongside their students.

Mary's words sent me on a quest to learn about the campaign in which volunteers who could read and write went into the factories and countryside to teach their fellow Cubans what they knew. Although the statistics vary from source to source, it is clear that more than 250,000 Cubans volunteered, and more than half of these were women and girls, who up until this time had lived quite limited, sheltered lives. Of the volunteer force, more than 100,000 were between the ages of ten and nineteen. The youngest volunteer was actually a seven-year-old girl who was assigned to teach an elderly neighbor. The oldest student was a woman who was 106 years old.

The campaign was announced by Fidel Castro in a speech he made at the United Nations in 1960. It was officially opened on January 28, 1961, and concluded on December 22 of that year. During that time, more than 700,000 Cubans learned to read and write. Representatives from the United Nations, who came to Cuba to consult with the educational leadership and observe the carrying out of the campaign, declared, at the end of 1961, that Cuba had achieved "universal literacy."

One of the most inspiring resources I encountered in my quest was the 2012 documentary *Maestra*, produced and directed by Catherine Murphy, which tells about the campaign through the stories of women who were Conrado Benítez Brigadistas as teenagers. All the women Murphy interviewed, now accomplished professionals in various fields, look back on the campaign of 1961 as the defining event of their lives. The companion book to the film, *A Year Without Sundays*, is a gold mine of detailed information, including quotations from many of the participants, the makeup of the campaign brigades, and even the words of the songs they sang. Many of the stories from the film and the book served as inspiration for Lora's story.

Another source upon which this book is dependent is Jonathan Kozol's *Children of the Revolution: A Yankee Teacher in the Cuban Schools* (New York: Delacorte, 1978). Kozol's book gives many valuable details of the campaign, including contents from the teacher and student books used and the tests given, even a sample letter to Fidel Castro — a wealth of material. I am particularly grateful to these three sources, but I am responsible for any factual errors in my book, including my attempts at Spanish translation.

In addition to the sources mentioned above, I owe a debt to Mark Abendroth's *Rebel Literacy: Cuba's National Literacy Campaign and Critical Global Citizenship* (Duluth, MN: Litwin, 2009). I am also grateful to Ann E. Halbert-Brooks for posting her 2013 master's thesis from the University of North Carolina at Chapel Hill, "Revolutionary Teachers: Women and Gender in the Cuban Literacy Campaign of 1961." I also gleaned much help from the Internet concerning Cuban history, geography, agriculture, flora, and fauna.

Thanks are also due to Leda Schubert, who, seeing my enthusiasm for the story, told me I should write about the campaign, and to Karen Lotz at Candlewick, who felt it was a story that young people in my own country would enjoy knowing. She is, as always, a gracious and perceptive editor. My friend Nancy Graff and my agent, Allison Cohen, read early drafts and gave me valuable suggestions and cheered me on. I hope they know how much I appreciate their help during those crucial stages. Also many thanks to my "special assistant," Aidan Sammis, who researched the time line, read the manuscript for all those typos and grammatical errors I seem to miss, and was the kind of help every disorganized writer wishes for and few have. And special thanks to Hannah Mahoney, for her thoughtful and careful copyediting of dates and facts, and the suggestions from both Karen and Hannah that were invaluable help in the final shaping of the story. I additionally would like to thank designers Sherry Fatla and Matt Roeser; talented mapmaker Mike Reagan; and jacket artist Rafael López, for his stunning illustration.

And, finally, thanks to the real-life Emilia and Isabel, who are two of the many reasons I have fallen in love with Cuba and the Cuban people.

My Brigadista Year is by no means intended to

be a full or balanced account of all events occurring in Cuba in the year 1961. Fidel Castro committed many evils against his enemies, some of whom originally fought on his side for freedom from Batista but felt betrayed by actions of the new government when small farms were seized and innocent families relocated or put in camps. From 1959 until his death, Castro presided over a repressive regime, jailing and executing political opponents and sometimes even those considered allies, and denying ordinary Cuban citizens freedoms we Americans take for granted. These freedoms include freedom of expression — widespread censorship, book banning, and even Bible burning have occurred in Cuba since Castro first assumed power. And the literacy campaign was not entirely staffed by idealistic volunteers like Lora. I understand that some families felt the pressure of potential reprisal for non-cooperation, and therefore, some young people might well have felt forced to join the campaign. As the year went on and the goal remained distant, schools were closed and teachers were also conscripted.

Yet it is true that Castro had a vision that basic literacy was important for a functioning society and for every Cuban citizen. Moreover, for decades Cubans have received universal free education and health care. It was an adventure for me as a writer to see the world through the eyes of a young person in a society quite different from my own. Through Lora's eyes, the revolution was a new day for her family and for a country that had long suffered under the corrupt dictatorship of Batista. She was excited to be a part of that new day, and as I wrote about her, so was I.

A Brief Time Line of Cuban History

Prehistory: According to archaeological remains, human habitation on the island now known as Cuba dates back to about 4000 BCE. The oldest known archaeological sites are the caves and rock shelters that were home to a people known as the Guanajatabey, who were hunter-gatherers, used stone tools, and made pictographs. Much later, by about 800 CE, they were also known to make pottery, probably as a result of interaction with other Caribbean peoples.

Probably around 400 BCE, the Arawak people began to spread out from Venezuela into the Caribbean. Among them were the Taíno, who arrived in Cuba around 300 CE. The Taíno brought agriculture with them and built villages centered around plazas, where ceremonies, festivals, and games were held. They grew cassava, which they ground into flour for bread, as well as cotton, tobacco, corn, and sweet potatoes. As Robert M. Poole has said, "If you have ever paddled a *canoe,* napped in a *hammock*, savored a *barbecue*, smoked *tobacco* or tracked a *hurricane* across *Cuba*, you have paid tribute to the Taíno" (*Smithsonian*, October 2011).

1492: Christopher Columbus claims Cuba for Spain.

1511: First Spanish settlements begin under the governorship of Diego Velázquez de Cuéllar. They are met by resistance from the indigenous Taíno leaders and people.

1512: Hatuey, a Taíno chief and resistance leader, is burned at the stake. Suffering through armed attacks and brutal mistreatment, as well as from new diseases introduced to Cuba by the colonizers, the native population is decimated over the next decades.

1526: Importation of enslaved people from Africa begins. Slave revolts begin shortly thereafter.

1607: Havana is named the capital of Cuba.

1717: In the first of three uprisings, tobacco growers protest the Spanish monopoly on the crop.

1762: Havana is occupied by the British during the Seven Years' War; Spain regains control of Cuba in 1763.

1807: The British end their slave trade and oppose Spain for its continuation.

1808: In parts of Spanish America, wars to end Spanish rule break out; they will last several decades. Many colonies will eventually declare independence.

1812: Slave revolts known as the Aponte Rebellion take place across Cuba.

1817: The Spanish monopoly on goods and trade in Cuba is abolished, opening the island to British, French, German, and later U.S. trade and investment. Cuba's sugar economy, fueled by massive importation of enslaved labor from Africa and indentured labor from China, will eventually supply 40 percent of the world's sugar.

1844: Uprisings against slavery and colonial rule are brutally suppressed during the "Year of the Lash."

1868: The Ten Years' War, the first war of Cuban independence, begins.

1870: Poet José Martí is sentenced to prison for writings considered treasonous by the colonial government; he is then pardoned and exiled to Spain.

1878: The Ten Years' War concludes with the Pact of Zanjón, which promises greater freedoms but not the end of slavery. Afro-Cuban General Antonio Maceo leads the Protest of Baraguá, rejecting the pact.

1879: General Maceo and others declare a second war, which ends in 1880; he and others are deported to Jamaica.

1886: Slavery is abolished in Cuba.

1892: Now living in the United States, Martí founds the Cuban Revolutionary Party among Cubans there in exile.

1895: Led by Martí, Maceo, and Dominican-born General Máximo Gómez y Báez, among others, the final war of independence begins. Martí is killed in battle just two days after landing in Cuba, but his political activity and his writings warning about the threat of Spanish and U.S. expansionism establish him as one of the great Latin-American intellectuals; he will come to be known as the "apostle of Cuban independence."

1898: In what came to be known as the Spanish-American War, the United States declares war on Spain following the sinking of the battleship USS *Maine* in Havana Harbor. Spain cedes control over Cuba, and the United States begins military occupation of the island.

1903: As a condition of ending its occupation, the United States ratifies the Platt Amendment, a rider to Cuba's constitutional sovereignty.

1906: The United States begins a second military occupation of Cuba; it will last until 1909.

1917: Cuba declares war on Germany, entering World War I on the side of the Allies.

The Russian Revolution reverberates around the world, including in Cuba.

1925: The first Communist Party of Cuba is founded, also to be known as the Popular Socialist Party.

1933: Fulgencio Batista leads the Revolt of the Sergeants, which topples the government.

1934: The Platt Amendment is repealed, and the United States relinquishes its right to involvement in Cuban internal affairs.

1940: Batista becomes president and establishes a new constitution.

1941: Cuba enters World War II by declaring war on Japan, Germany, and Italy.

1944: Batista retires and is succeeded by President Ramón Grau San Martín.

1952: Batista overthrows the elected government and

becomes a corrupt dictator with close ties to the U.S. Mafia.

1953: Fidel Castro leads a revolt against the Batista regime. Although the attack is unsuccessful, it inspires the 26th of July Movement and is considered the beginning of the Cuban Revolution. Castro is jailed but eventually released and leaves for Mexico, where he continues to muster revolutionary forces.

1956: Fidel Castro, his brother Raúl, the Argentinian revolutionary Ernesto "Che" Guevara, and a small band of guerrillas land in Cuba. Most of the group are killed, but a few make their way into the Sierra Maestra mountain range, where they recruit, rearm, and initiate a guerrilla war against Batista's government. Because of strict censorship of the news, most Cubans are unaware that Fidel is still alive or that the 26th of July guerrillas are winning the war against Batista's forces.

1959: In January, Castro and the rebels triumphantly enter Havana; Castro becomes prime minister, with his brother Raúl as commander in chief. All U.S.

businesses in Cuba are eventually nationalized by the Cuban government.

1961: The United States breaks off diplomatic relations with Cuba. A U.S.-sponsored invasion by counter-revolutionaries at the Bay of Pigs is quickly defeated by the Cuban military.

The Cuban Literacy Campaign to abolish illiteracy raises the official literacy rate from approximately 60 percent to 96 percent within one year. United Nations observers declare Cuba an "illiteracy-free" nation.

Castro declares Cuba a socialist state and develops an alliance with the Soviet Union. Many upper and middle-class Cubans leave for the United States.

1962: The United States imposes an embargo on Cuba.

The Cuban Missile Crisis, a confrontation between the United States and the Soviet Union over the placement of Soviet missiles in Cuba, brings the two powers close to nuclear war.

1965: The Communist Party of Cuba, the only official political party, is formally established. There is another exodus of Cubans to the United States.

1976: The 1976 constitution institutionalizes the principals of the Cuban Revolution; Fidel Castro becomes president.

The flow of people northward continues. Some who leave Cuba fear repression from the government and seek political asylum in the United States; others leave for economic reasons as the Cuban economy falters through the 1970s and 1980s.

1980: Tensions between the United States and Cuba over immigration come to a head, leading to the Mariel boatlift.

1982: President Ronald Reagan adds Cuba to the U.S. list of state sponsors of terrorism for its support of revolutionary movements in Latin America and Africa.

1991: The Cuban economy suffers after the collapse of the Soviet Union and a tightening of the U.S. embargo.

1994: A crisis arises when Castro announces that anyone who wants to leave Cuba may do so. People take to the Florida straits on rafts and small, unseaworthy boats. Many lives are lost.

2002: A museum dedicated to exploring and preserving the history of the Taíno people opens in Baracoa.

2004: The first census to investigate current-day Taíno descendants is announced.

2008: Fidel Castro retires and Raúl Castro takes over as president, promising to consult his older brother on all important matters. Relations with the European Union, Russia, and China begin to improve.

2011: Reforms encouraging private enterprise are approved by the Cuban government.

2013: Raúl Castro is reelected by the National Assembly and says he will stand down in 2018.

2015: The United States removes Cuba from its list of states that sponsor terrorism. Cuba and the United

States reopen embassies, and some travel and trade restrictions are eased.

2016: U.S. president Barack Obama visits Cuba, raising hopes for a new era of improved diplomatic and economic relations, though the embargo remains in place.

Fidel Castro dies at age ninety.

2017: U.S. president Donald Trump announces a rollback of recently improved U.S.-Cuba relations.

Raúl Castro's Communist regime continues. Cuba's literacy rate remains one of the highest in the world, variously reported as 99.75 percent to 99.9 percent.